The Separation of Walter Crane

Derek Steffen

—

First paperback edition February 2023
Cover Design by GetCovers

Independently Published

ISBN 9798373651615

—

To my kids,
for their continual inspiration and occasional patience.

Chapter 1

Walter Crane sits in the back corner of the school bus with his head down and anxiety up. While his fourth-grade classmates bounce off the vehicle's torn-leather upholstery, their volume dials turned all the way to the right, Walter silently counts. On any other day, the drive from Richfield Elementary to the California Railroad Museum would take ten minutes. Thanks to a malfunctioning light rail crossing arm, the trip is at the twenty-five-minute mark, 1,500 seconds by Walter's count. Walter counts to block out the bullies that see his crooked teeth and thick glasses as a constant target. Today his tormentors are the usual suspects, Terrence Johns and Freddy Robinson.

Terrence and Freddy first caught sight of Walter while road workers serviced the broken transit arm. The two bullies then exchanged whispers and a pair of mischievous smiles. As an ovation celebrated the crossing arm's repair, the boys darted from their seats and into the bus' back corner. They were Walter's new benchmates before the applause ended. 672, 673, 674 . . .

When you are as routinely picked on as Walter has been this year, you focus less on the specific actions of your attack and more on its duration. *When will this end? Why is this not over yet?* It is like a terrible song that seems to add a new verse whenever it plays. The insults. The crowding. The elbowing. The kicking of shins. Walter's decision to hide in the corner afforded him safety at first, but it also put him in the blind spot of any would-be savior. With no one coming to the rescue, Walter concentrated on the fabric lining of his pants pockets. 823, 824, 825 . . .

Before Walter could reach 900, his assailants returned to their original seats. The lack of any good reaction bored them. Unfortunately, Walter missed this development as he kept counting, kept thrashing his fingers against his pockets' boundaries, and kept his eyes closed to present himself with at least one reality where the worst possible was not the most likely. Walter had long envisioned the dismissal bell on the last day of school—only a week away—as his moment of release but would now settle for Ms. Meadows' impending announcement of, "Okay, we're here. Everyone off."

Richfield was not a new school, Terrence and Freddy were not new classmates, but fourth grade had gone differently than any year previous. It began in the summer when Walter's adult teeth started to come in at an off-kilter angle. He eventually visited an orthodontist but found out it would be years before he was eligible for braces. This was tragic news for him but a blessing for his mother, Elizabeth, who had more time to gather the $6,000 necessary for the procedure, a feat all the harder to accomplish on a single paycheck. Walter's dad had been struck dead by a reckless driver three days before Thanksgiving. Then worsening astigmatism and stilt-like limbs were issues come Christmas.

While his physical challenges brought embarrassment, the loss of his father brought isolation, and Walter started to believe that somehow he had brought it all on himself. He tried to think of every conceivable reason why his ordinary life had fallen apart so spectacularly. Was it the time he swore at his grandma's house? Was it the Halloween candy he snuck every year? Or was it simply him—something innately wrong with him? Academically, Walter was successful at school. Socially, he had always managed. Lately, however, he had become an expert at counting in his head.

2582, 2583, 2584—

"Okay, we're here. Everyone off."

***

God bless the tour guides. God bless the volunteers who raise their hands when asked who wants to herd nine-year-olds on a trip through history. There are no assigned seats. There are 360 degrees of new distractions. Still, there are those docents who bravely take school children by the bus-full and attempt to leave them with a bit of knowledge and lore.

The two gathered 4th-grade classes are split into six different sections this morning. Each group has one adult chaperone, one museum guide, and ten students. Because Walter's misfortune never takes a day off, he finds himself in a group with Terrence and Freddy. He is not sure how this happened. It makes no sense alphabetically, as there are enough letters between them that he should have been safe by first name or last. At a minimum, he should have been safe from both boys.

Walter's strategy for survival is to stay as close as possible to his adult chaperone, Ms. Meadows. While occasionally oblivious, Ms. Meadows also has been an ally, providing Walter refuge in the form of books from her library. As he stands alongside his teacher, the group facing their docent and her body blocking him from any potential assassins, Walter is at peace.

Those mammoth locomotives, mighty relics of yesterday's travels, have the students spellbound. They suck up the guide's quaint delivery of historical context at every syllable. That is until they reach the museum's showpiece, The Golden Spike, and Katie Jennings informs Ms. Meadows that she has to go pee.

"That's real gold," the guide wows his captive audience. The ceremonial spike from the completion of the

Transcontinental Railroad shines in all their eyes. "Over 150 years ago, this spike was driven into the ground. It was in celebration—"

"Ms. Meadows, I have to go to the bathroom," Katie whispers to her teacher. Students were encouraged to use the facilities back at school. While it was a miracle that the extended bus ride had not produced any dramatic pleas to pee earlier, staff made sure to point out the restrooms once they set foot in the museum. Katie Jennings, however, had been too caught up in a side conversation to think ahead.

Fortunately for Ms. Meadows, there is a bathroom not far from her current position. She hates to leave Walter, whom she intentionally put into her group, but fate in the form of a fourth-grader doing the toilet two-step has intervened. (She also purposefully selected Terrence and Freddy, as it did not seem fair to pawn them off on an unsuspecting parent.)

Before parting with Katie, Ms. Meadows peers down at Walter, sweet, clueless Walter. He comes off like a gangly cartoon mouse, the lovable if not pathetic kind featured in holiday TV specials. Ms. Meadows speaks to him in a soft tone perfected by only the best teachers, "Walter, I'm going to take Katie to the bathroom. Do you need to go?"

Walter, who is in the process of committing the measurements of the spike to memory, politely shakes his head "no." Ms. Meadows gives him a look that says, "this is for your own good," but Walter does not blink. She accepts the boy's desire to learn and hustles Katie off to fulfill the commitment the young girl made that morning to her chocolate milk.

Bullies sense weakness intuitively, so it does not take long to happen. Terrence and Freddy notice their teacher leaving, and as though a cloud has moved from the sun, they look at Walter and see opportunity. When later asked why they did it, the two will offer little explanation. *He started it. He was staring at us. He's a know-it-all.* Resentment is more easily accessed at a younger age than self-awareness ever is.

As the tour guide walks on to the next exhibit, he puts his back to the children and the spike. Walter moves to take one last look at all that glittering history, and, in this moment of separation, Terrence and Freddy close in on him. Nuzzled against the barrier rope that places the spike just beyond reach, Walter hangs his arms calmly while on either side awaits his future. He is as blind to the bullies as he is blind to the action that will forever alter him, his family, and his hometown.

"Ass face, it looks like they pulled that spike from your ugly mouth."

Walter is shocked back to reality by Freddy's remark. He turns around to face his firing squad. They load their ammunition.

"Ms. Meadows is gone, so there's no one to save you now."

Walter starts counting.

"Aw, look at the little coward close his eyes. *Little coward.*"

Back on the bus, the turtle routine got the better of his classmates, but they will not be so quickly done away with this time. They need to satiate their primal desires. They need to see blood spilled.

It starts with Freddy's knee to Walter's groin. Not good enough. He is still standing. *Spit.* Terrence spits in Walter's face. His eyes remain shut tight. Walter is not here. This is not happening. He has transported himself back to the bus, back to the morning, back to the nighttime pizza run his father took in November, back to the vacation his family took to Lake Tahoe not long after his sister's birth. Now the calendar's pages move faster. Decades peel off in milliseconds. Centuries are gone. Walter stands in a crowd of hundreds. It's 1859. Leland Stanford builds momentum and drives a golden spike into the track. A metallic sound pierces through the gathered onlookers as a metallic thud interrupts the museum today. In a struggle to snatch his glasses, Walter's head has been palmed and shoved backward, colliding with an awful smack of violence against the jutting top of the spike. Terrence and Freddy get their blood.

Chapter 2

It has been six months since Elizabeth Crane was last in a hospital. With Thanksgiving imminent and neither she nor her husband in the mood to cook, he volunteered to pick up dinner. The drive to Giant Pizza and back should have taken twenty minutes, twenty-five at most. When forty minutes passed, and she had not received a text, Elizabeth thought it odd but not dire. Anyway, her two boys were knee-deep in school vacation, while her youngest, Annie, was running and jumping into the couch as recklessly as ever, so there were enough distractions to keep her from worrying. Then the call came, the vague instructions from an unfamiliar voice to get down to Leidesdorff Memorial as soon as possible. She wasn't sure how long she would be gone, so Elizabeth grabbed her keys and put her eldest, Mitchell, in charge. She would be right back, she promised. Mitchell smiled wide with the privilege of responsibility, Walter whined, and Annie dove headfirst into nearby cushions.

When Elizabeth pulled up to the emergency entrance, she followed directions through a series of doors, eventually arriving at a glass partition. She expected to find her husband on the opposite side of the glass with a grin that asked, "What took so long?"; instead, she saw only his outline obscured by men and women in scrubs and constant motion. In time, Elizabeth could see her husband's face, but no wry expression materialized. He lay motionless, expressionless, gone.

This morning, the call comes from Ms. Meadows. This morning, the directions are to the Leidesdorff Pediatric Care Unit. This morning, Elizabeth drives up not expecting a short visit but prepared for doom. Doom is an abstraction used to protect from anything too specific. It is all the emotional wagering she can manage. Anything more would be too concrete. Anything more would be considering the death of a child, and how can she consider that?

***

Elizabeth stares at Walter as she pushes tears aside with a tissue and holds on to him with her other hand. If it were not for all the gadgets in the room and the bed propped up at a fifty-degree angle, Walter's resting face would suggest a state of normality. The staples in his head are not visible, the effects of his concussion are not outwardly noticeable, and the trauma is not immediately apparent. But then you pull back and take in the heart monitor, take in the whiteboard that reads "scalp laceration," and take in the parental sense of dread plastered all over Elizabeth's face, and this cannot be normal. *This can't be happening.* How many times did Walter come home and complain of being picked on? How many phone calls did she make? How many emails did she write? *Not enough,* Elizabeth thinks. Being a parent is trying to fight off the reality that there are limits to what you can do.

When Elizabeth claims she does not have a favorite child, she is mostly telling the truth. Annie is her wild one, Mitchell is her future president, but Walter is purely hers: her toughest pregnancy, the one who most reminds her of herself, and the only one of her three not to look exactly like their dad. While Elizabeth is gratified by the ways Walter resembles her, she also finds the resemblance frightening. As she remembers the waves of emotions that beset her as a kid, fragile and stumbling through adolescence, Elizabeth cannot remember how she survived.

The Posey sisters were Elizabeth's particular schoolyard agitators. They would come on campus brandishing new vocabulary like a sharpened saber. "Peon" was a particular weapon of choice one day. The elder Posey had picked up the term from a history book, and the girls used it to attack Elizabeth during the following recess. Her sister, Carol, went to the same school but was too young to even numbers up, so Elizabeth was left exposed, a nervous bookworm with no true allies. Over time, she began to accept the Poseys' insults as fact, internalizing every cruel word thrown her way. Therapy and a supportive partner eventually overpowered the damage done on the playground, but those insecurities have reemerged in the six months since her husband's death. Now, as Elizabeth clasps Walter's skinny fingers in her anxious palm, she wonders where she went wrong and if he will ever forgive her.

The television is turned on in the background to provide a counter to the eerie silence of Walter's room. Machines beep occasionally and only intensify Elizabeth's nerves. Things never quieted down like this in the emergency room with her husband. She knows a freeway and busy downtown streets are on the other side of the nearby window. Morbidly, she marvels at how thick and sealed the window must be to keep all that noise away. The TV drones on. A car insurance commercial. A machine beeps. A local news report about the homeless. Walter, she has been assured, is out of danger. There will be side effects, and the doctors want to be cautious, but the MRI looked good. External bleeding was stopped quickly. No internal bleeding was detected. Elizabeth knows rest is what Walter needs most, but she also desperately wants him to wake up and say her name.

Not long after yet another ad for low-rate auto coverage, Elizabeth gets her wish. "Mom." Walter is too groggy to say anything else. It will be another ten minutes of near-waking up before he fully can. He sucks water through a straw, takes a slow gulp, and speaks again, "Mom." His speech is slurred, but she hears him clearly.

"Hey, babe. I'm here. How are you feeling?"

Walter isn't sure how he is feeling. "Where are Mitchell and Annie?"

"Mitchell is still at school. I dropped your sister off with Aunt Carol."

"You're by yourself?" Walter asks in a concerned manner that makes him sound like the parent.

"I'm here with you, babe. Do you know what happened?"

No response is given. Walter is equal parts aware and unsure of what occurred. He knows he is hurt. He is smart enough to understand that from the fear draped over his mother. The hospital setting is a dead giveaway too. He remembers Terrence and Freddy, but what could they have done to put him in this position? *I'm only a kid. Why am I here?*

Pushing past Walter's non-answer, Elizabeth proceeds, "Are you hungry? Do you want to talk?" The boy's head passively shakes side-to-side as Elizabeth struggles with her sudden bystander status. "Okay, if you want to talk, just talk. I'm here."

In Elizabeth's movie version of events, Walter leaps out of bed and into her arms. The pair embrace as the credits roll. However, back in the sterile confines of the hospital room, the boy searches through the fog for a response, "Mom, do I have to go back to school?"

***

The Cranes have long outgrown their house in downtown Sacramento. They are four in a two-bedroom, bittersweetly with more space than when Walter's father was alive. Elizabeth contemplated moving after her husband's passing, but with so much instability already present in the household, she did not believe it wise. *They have already lost their father, so why should they also lose the only home they've ever known?*

Mr. and Mrs. Crane moved in as newlyweds. It was the first time signing their names together on a lease, and the house felt massive. When Mitchell was born shortly after, he took over the second bedroom, and his toys began to soak up previously open real estate. Still, it was manageable. Then came Walter, and free space became a rarity. While Walter now shares a room and bunk beds with Mitchell, it took Elizabeth some convincing to consent to this arrangement. She spent the weeks following his birth visiting the hospital every day, unable to take him home. Doctors detected fluid in his lungs, which necessitated an extended stay at the NICU. Once Walter was discharged, the Cranes' original plan was for him to spend the first year in a crib in their room before moving him down the hallway with his brother. That first year blurred into several more before Elizabeth finally agreed to let Walter out of her immediate sight.

Years after this challenging transition, Annie was born healthy and active but without a room to call her own. The Cranes immediately identified in their daughter an independence that set her apart from Walter. Even after moving down the hallway, Walter walked into his parents' bedroom at night when he felt anxious. He would tiptoe to the side of his sleeping mother, his whispers rousing her and nearby Annie. Then Elizabeth would coax her two youngest back to bed, sometimes through the satisfaction of a midnight snack. All the while, Walter's dad snoozed on, his dedication to slumber only rivaled in the household by Mitchell.

Throughout the many hard nights since last November, those cross-hallway visits have grown in frequency; however, instead of leading Walter back to his room, Elizabeth has given in and allowed him to sleep on the side of the bed once occupied by her late husband. Because Mitchell and Annie possess natural survival skills, she does not worry about them the same. On the other hand, she sleeps better knowing that Walter sleeps better next to her. When contemplating a change of scenery, Elizabeth wonders if the hallways in their next house will also creak to tell her that Walter is on his way.

Aside from space issues, there is an ongoing contest for attention. After Annie's birth, Walter went from youngest child to middle child, a demotion that has left him feeling like a castaway. "Why does Annie get to stay with you when she's in trouble, but I get sent upstairs?"

"She doesn't have her own room."

"I don't have my own room."

"You have your room with your brother."

"It's not my own. But I still have to go there when I'm in trouble."

"Your room is a kid's room. You can be there by yourself. Annie doesn't have that, so she can't."

"How come she gets to cuddle with you?"

"Do you want to cuddle with me?"

"Sometimes."

"When?"

"When I get home from school."

"When you're supposed to be doing your homework?"

"And she gets new toys."

"You have plenty of toys."

"Mitchell's toys."

"They're for both of you."

"But they were his toys first."

"Your sister is much younger than you, so she has different toys."

Walter's big lips quiver as he stomps away. He cannot downplay the emotion in his voice, no matter how stoic he tries to be. The tears streaming past his fogged-up glasses are also an obvious tell. At first, the family took these crying fits as a positive—a sign his lungs were finally in working order—but now the franticness appears to have no end. On school mornings, when Elizabeth tells her kids they have to leave in three minutes and need to finish their breakfast ASAP, Walter is the one who turns red as he begins shoveling food in his mouth.

"Walter, calm down."

"But you said three minutes. I won't have enough time."

"You'll be fine. Just calm down."

Raising any kid is a gamble. Raising Walter has been like highwire walking over rapids infested with sharks and self-doubt. Elizabeth has to pick her battles carefully. Is she willing to die on the hill marked "slow eater"? Or is it something else? With all this cautious treading she does for Walter's sake, she finds it all the more surprising when he approaches one morning, not long after his recent hospital stay, to announce, "I don't want you to treat me like a baby anymore."

Walter's lips are not quivering. His theory is as follows: "Everyone sees me as weak. They know I share a room. They know my little sister bosses me around. They know that Dad is gone. They see me with glasses. They see my teeth. They hear how you talk to me. They hear how all the teachers talk to me. So they pick on me because they know they can get away with it. Terrence and Freddy are going to get away with it. Nothing's going to happen to them. I'm the only one something happens to. Everything happens to me. And I don't want it anymore."

Elizabeth's response is as follows: *What!?!*

Mitchell once spent a three-day weekend at a friend's house. When he returned, Elizabeth thought his voice sounded deeper than before. She checked on him later that night to find him barely contained by his twin mattress. Then, last spring, Annie started to use multisyllabic words that she picked up from overheard song lyrics. She talked about how she needed to be "hydrated" or only wanted naps in "moderation." Elizabeth reacted the same in both instances: eyes wide, jaw open, *where did my babies go?*

In contrast, Walter has been consistent. Walter has never left her side. He is a longer version of his younger self but still that little boy at heart. She can look at him and see his whole story: in his eyes, his posture, the way he starts his sentences. That's how it always has been.

Now Walter is having his turn, Elizabeth thinks. Her little whimpering pup has begun to growl, and she is unsure if she is scared more by how shocking it all is or how believable it all feels. *Yes,* she admits to herself, *I coddle you, but that's only to make up for the times I didn't get to hold you when you were first born. And, yes, I let you sleep in the bed with me because I don't do well by myself, but the same goes for you. How come Annie and Mitchell aren't like this? What did I do wrong? What just happened?*

These questions remain backstage. In the recent past, a hug would solve everything, but when Elizabeth can finally blink again, she only manages a bashful "okay." The word choice appeases Walter but stings her. Letting go of old practices is going to take practice.

Later that night, after things have settled, Elizabeth approaches her son as though nothing has changed, as though a time traveler did not crash on their doorstep mere hours before. She is optimistic, "So tomorrow I think we should do the *trifecta.* It's been a while since we've done that."

The "trifecta" refers to the three kid-centric attractions in the nearby neighborhood of Land Park: the Sacramento Zoo, Fairytale Town, and Funderland. The animal sanctuary, the storybook-themed park, and Funderland, home to the area's only year-round rides and roller coaster, are the type of places designed for a surge in adolescent adrenaline and dopamine levels. The Cranes typically make their way to one location per outing, maybe two in a day if daring, but they have not attempted the trifecta in years. Hours of outside running in Sacramento's oppressive heat are not for the weak-willed. While the sun is not his concern, the look on Walter's face suggests that he is not a fan of the idea.

"Mom. I told you I don't want to be treated like a baby anymore."

"How is the zoo for babies?"

"Is there anything to do there that I couldn't do when I was Annie's age?"

"You're too grown-up for lions? And what about how much we laughed the last time we saw the chimps?"

"That was like two years ago. I was younger then."

"You're not that old now."

"Too old for Fairytale Town."

"Okay. I will give you that, but don't you remember when you were your Annie's age? I took you all the time back then. It doesn't seem fair that she can never go again because you've started to feel old."

Suddenly, Mitchell bellows across the house, sounding like he has a mouth full of chips, "They put the Robin Hood stuff in too!"

Elizabeth turns towards the hallway and scolds, "Mitchell. Your mouth. Finish chewing." She then swivels back towards Walter, "They have the Robin Hood stuff too."

Walter considers and then relents, "Fine. Fairytale Town is fine—we can do that for Annie."

"And don't tell me you don't want to do the dragon ride at Funderland."

Walter poorly tries to cover a smile, "Fairytale and Funderland. Okay."

Elizabeth smiles back, tension turning away. "See. I knew you'd come around. And then can we at least do the zoo for me?"

"Why do you like that place so much?"

"The giraffes."

"What's so special about them?"

"They get to stand around all day in the shade and eat."

"So?"

"You'll understand when you get older." Elizabeth winks. Walter groans. Tomorrow is set.

Chapter 3

There are those things that happen. They just happen. No one notices. Then something else happens. A moment comes and goes and only returns to mind when later events point to its significance. For Walter Crane, it starts with a pile of toys.

Annie is playing the way Annie always plays. She finds a group of toys, fidgets with them briefly, and at the end is left with a mound of brightly colored plastic. Then she immediately declares she is done "playing" and ready to clean up. Tonight there are multiple groups of toys: princesses, dinosaurs, planes, musical instruments, cars, jewelry, and a handful of magnets for good measure. The mound has become mountainous. Elizabeth would customarily have interjected once the toy strands began intermixing; however, a day of workshops at her job as a librarian has left her without much inclination to interrupt her daughter's graceful chaos. She is too busy daydreaming about giraffes anyway.

"Where are my crowns?" R-controlled words challenge Annie's tongue, though she seems not to mind. There, unfortunately, is no answer to her question. Elizabeth is sprawled on the couch, and Walter is tucked in a corner, reading a graphic novel while Mitchell plays on his tablet. Annie is not pleased. She repeats herself, this time more forcefully. Through closed eyes, Elizabeth instructs Mitchell to assist his sister.

Mitchell responds, "Why can't Walter? He's the one that wants to be a grown-up."

Giraffes eat 65 pounds per day.

After a few seconds of awkward silence followed by Annie's patented snarl, Walter begrudgingly comes to the rescue. He sets down his book and walks over to the landfill of trinkets and figurines that has become the living room. Mitchell's eyes never move from his device, but Elizabeth sits up. The relationship between Annie and Walter has historically been tenuous. She is an alpha. He is whoever gets devoured by the alpha.

"What do you need, Annie?"

"Okay, Walter, this is a conversation." Annie speaks like she has taken an English immersion class at night school.

"An important conversation," Walter affirms.

"Walter! I was talking my conversation! I can't find my crown." Annie has a quick trigger.

"Sorry. Your tiara, the one you can wear?"

"Yes. My tee-awww-uh. Yes, yes, yes."

Elizabeth intervenes, "I think she's talking about the one that goes with her princess toys. The one she can wear is upstairs in the dress-up stuff."

Walter surveys the mess before him to determine the best place to begin. The toy pile is multiple feet wide, while the tiara in question is several inches long at most. There are likely whole animal species and a track's worth of race cars covering the elusive crown. As Walter sits, Annie walks over to place her hand on his shoulder.

"Annie, are you actually going to play with it if I find it for you?"

"Yes. It's my favorite in the whole wide world."

"Alright. I'll do it."

Annie shows Walter her gratitude by leaning over from behind to hug him. Her left cheek dives down and into the back of his head, colliding into the spot that once met The Golden Spike. Walter winces and reaches for the source of irritation, checking for blood that, thankfully, is not there. Annie adjusts. The thing has just happened.

When Walter places his hand on the rubble, intending to move a felt panda out of the way, he winces once more, and the panda falls from his loosening grip. *Weird*, he thinks. Mitchell remains glued to his screen. Elizabeth is back to considering how many pounds of food she can consume in a day, while Annie has started her dig on the periphery.

Walter regroups. This time when he grasps the panda, he drives his hand firmly down, ensuring that his fingers can secure it from every side. As he pushes, toys slowly, clumsily ripple in all directions. Before Walter can pull his hand up and drop the cushioned bamboo-eater out of the way, his eyes reflexively shut, and a murmur of an image flashes. Walter purposefully drops the animal. He reviews the last minute and then scans his family for reactions. Nothing. *What's going on*? Walter considers asking aloud, but he is unsure how to explain it to himself, let alone anyone else in the room.

For his final attempt, Walter plunges his hand a few deliberate inches deeper before his eyes shut again, and the vision returns. Initially, there are shimmering, yellowish scamps of light followed by the snow from an old TV, flecks of black scurrying in circles. In the center is a streaming silver beacon, expanding in size until it covers Walter's entire field of vision. Without realizing it, his hand begins to change course abruptly. Walter leans over the pile, his fingers pulling him forward and then down, the silver light pulsing and generating heat. Walter struggles to open his eyes. Suddenly, the swelling of action stops, and he can see the room. It returns to focus as Walter looks down at his hand. He is holding a small plastic crown. No one has noticed.

***

The sign posted at the entrance of Fairytale Town's Crooked Mile clearly states, "NO RUNNING." However, how can such a policy be enforced when hyperactive kids, most of whom cannot read or do not care to acknowledge the sign, are the attraction's target audience? The Crooked Mile is a five-minute winding pathway in the middle of towering plant life, allowing the illusion that this is a magical land where the outside world of parents and caution does not exist: what you cannot see, you do not consider. So kids run and jog and train for future Olympic glory through its twists and turns, while the physically frail or emotionally apprehensive either stay away or require a chaperone. The slender design of The Crooked Mile adds layers of intrigue to such arrangements, as child-parent hand-holding is hard to manage on its narrow trails. For this reason, Walter again offers to assist his sister.

Annie is not emotionally reticent, but her size does put her at a disadvantage among the throngs of rapidly moving older and bigger bodies. Elizabeth and Mitchell have played hand-holder on more than one occasion, but Walter chooses to be his sister's guide today because he needs to distract himself. He needs to switch his focus from the swirling thoughts in his head that remind him of how helpless and confused he felt last night when a light show took over his eyes. The episode kept him up an extra two hours in bed. He wanted to talk to Mitchell about it, but Mitchell, a champion slumberer, was in mid-season form. Walter wanted to crawl into his mom's bed and unburden himself as usual, but he felt this would betray his earlier speech; instead, he stayed awake, allowing inadequate explanations to churn inside his brain and eventually tire him out.

The first thing Walter notices about The Crooked Mile is that too many kids are here. They do not understand the need for space or even simple sidewalk decorum. It's like somebody let a bag of bouncy balls fall from a ten-story building—this is madness. At a certain point, Annie is leading, and Walter is holding on dearly. Elizabeth did not say anything earlier, but Walter always chose to skip this particular attraction when he was younger. He was built more to water Mr. McGregor's Garden and survey King Arthur's Castle. What appeals to most about The Crooked Mile—its many lefts and rights and ups and downs and its disconnect from life beyond the plant perimeter—distresses Walter. As he reaches its final steps with his sister and returns to the safety of the ground, his hands sweating and face blushing red, he decides he is finished playing big brother for the afternoon.

***

The Cranes walk across the street to their next stop, Funderland. There are only nine rides, but the low-key atmosphere entices local families. A road trip to a more renowned theme park may offer greater thrills, but Funderland's simplicity is a happy alternative, particularly without high costs or long lines.

After picking up their wristbands, Walter and Mitchell head straight for The Chinese Dragon as Annie and Elizabeth make their way to The Octopus. The dragon coaster presents twists and turns and dips and dives similar to The Crooked Mile and at much greater speeds, but Walter is calm here. He gains a sense of certainty from the gravity that powers the roller coaster and the seatbelt fastened snugly around his waist. Predictability is a balm for the often-worrying mind.

Walter's mouth opens as the ride starts, and a yelp of excitement escapes. He and Mitchell will stay on five times in a row. During ride three, Elizabeth comes over to check on her boys. She sees Walter's eyes, alive, unencumbered by their usual tension. Elizabeth often frets about how he doesn't enjoy things the way his peers do and how his joys always seem to come quietly, never louder than turning a page in a book. While she loves how unique Walter is, watching him scream and smile like every other kid on the ride, she loves this side of him too. Elizabeth wants him to have the childhood she had but also the one she never got to know.

***

A Lavender Albino Reticulated Python slinks around, searching for a meal at the Sacramento Zoo's Reptile House. Patterns befitting a tye-dye shirt lead to lines of brown that streak towards the snake's tool-shaped head. On either side of its head lie powerful eyes that stare at Walter as he whispers, "Wow!" He does not remember this animal from previous visits. The Reptile House was built when the zoo and Sacramento had smaller numbers. It fills up fast. Today, fortunately, it is sparsely attended and a well-received pause from the punishing sun outside.

Reptiles, especially with their cunning adaptations, have always fascinated Walter. He imagines the heft of the twenty-foot python, how cold it is to the touch, how unassuming it appears, but how quickly it can go from zero to kill if needed. Annie is unclear why it doesn't have ears. "They have an ear inside their heads," Walter tells her.

"But how do they hear things?" the little girl wonders.

Walter looks to his mom to explain "sound is vibration" to a three-year-old.

"Annie, when something bad tries to get a snake, it can listen to the footsteps on the ground. It can feel the sound it makes. That's how it hears," Elizabeth offers.

While he takes a slight exception to the word "footsteps," Walter is satisfied. "And, Annie, they can actually forecast if an earthquake is coming because of this," he adds.

Earthquake? Forecast? Annie loses interest and moves on. Elizabeth notices, "Last stop at the giraffes, and then how about some ice cream from Vic's?"

The trio approves.

***

As Elizabeth stands on the raised giraffe platform, she is envious of the animals' leisure. Annie stands next to her, trying to learn how the platform's metal bars feel against her cheek. Suddenly, a shriek of pain erupts from behind. Elizabeth instantly recognizes Walter's voice and turns to see him lying face-first on the pavement below. Mitchell is crouched over his brother, one hand on Walter's back. With Annie on her hip, Elizabeth races over, "What happened? Walter, are you hurt?"

"We were playing tag. He tripped. It was an accident," Mitchell answers.

Elizabeth glares at the word "tag," an issue of much contention in the house. However, now is not the time to drag that conversation back out again. "Mitchell, go watch your sister," Elizabeth instructs. Mitchell obliges, and Walter and Elizabeth are left together. A milling crowd of onlookers disperses. "Walter, I'm here. Do you want to try and move into the shade?"

"No, it hurts too bad," he whimpers.

"Where does it hurt? Your head?"

"My hands, my arms."

Elizabeth exhales. *Anything but his head.*

"Babe, you have to remember to breathe." Walter had forgotten. The whimpers turn down a notch. "Do you want to say my name?" Off in the background, a giraffe snorts. "It's me. You can say it."

Years ago, when Walter's anxiety first flared up, he saw a child psychologist who told him about the calming power of the "m" sound. During exceptionally rough waves of agitation, he was encouraged to take deep breaths in and out and then repeat an *m-word* of his choosing. The psychologist had suggested the word "calm," while Elizabeth thought an "ohm" chant might do the trick. Walter decided for himself: "mom." It was a sweet moment and had been a helpful tool; however, a day removed from a lecture on his budding maturity, chanting "mom" feels like a step backward. Instead, Walter takes three more breaths and then picks himself off the ground, leaving behind a few drops of blood from his right wrist.

"Is he okay?" Joel wears a small puff of an afro, a high school volunteer looking to build his résumé with a summer job.

"A couple scrapes, not too bad," Elizabeth responds.

"You alright, champ?" Joel asks Walter directly.

"Yeah. Tripped over a crack. I'll be fine."

"That's good. You know, they're actually planning on repaving the walkway." Joel misses Elizabeth's twisted face of a response and carries on, "Yeah, the zoo just hired a new director. They're fixing up a lot."

Back in congenial mode, Elizabeth smiles approvingly. "That's good, but Walter, here, is my tough guy—"

"Mom!" Now Walter says it, but this time with a horrified look attached.

Joel smiles and continues, "Well, if it's alright, I would like to take down your information so we can check on everything in a few days."

Numbers are exchanged. Walter cannot feel his cuts, only the twinge of embarrassment. He wants to save himself before leaving. "Hey, did you know there's something buried under there?"

Joel turns back to Walter. "What's that, champ?"

"Where I fell. Under the ground, there's a metal box or something." No one is quite sure what to say. Walter senses from the silence he needs to explain further. "I could see it when I fell. When they redo the ground, just tell them to be careful."

The silence is mercifully broken a second later. "Sure. I can do that. Thanks for the tip." Joel is dismissive in the gentlest way possible, "Have a nice day."

As the Cranes walk back, Walter brushes his hanging skin away. Mitchell stares, Annie names every flavor of ice cream she knows, and Elizabeth searches for the best way to ask her next question. "Walter, why did you tell that man you saw a box under the ground?"

"Because I did."

Chapter 4

Elizabeth Crane misses how impersonal her landline telephone was. She could screen calls, turn the ringer down, or even unhook the phone from the jack and not feel like it was such a sacrifice. However, shutting off a cellphone feels like a betrayal of obligations; nevertheless, there are those instances when it becomes necessary to disconnect from the modern world. In these moments, Elizabeth places her device in airplane mode, sets it out of sight, and goes off with her kids. When the need to escape ends, she turns her phone back on and clenches her teeth as she awaits the forthcoming deluge of communication. This is the scene when a voicemail from the zoo pops up. The caller sounds curious, a little mysterious, as she asks Elizabeth to call back at her earliest convenience. *One voicemail from the zoo—not bad.* Elizabeth does not know how impactful this one call will be.

It has been six weeks since The Cranes' trifecta run. Elizabeth has been to four workshops in that time, Mitchell has beaten three video games, Annie has written her name successfully twice, and Walter has dreaded going back to school every day. While Elizabeth cannot guarantee an end to the bullying, she promises to do everything to ensure her son's safety: "I won't let anything else happen to you. I'm going to meet with the principal and your teacher before the school year even starts. We are going to have a plan."

"But what if that plan doesn't work?"

"But what if it does? We don't know what will happen. Anyway, we can't afford to homeschool, and I want you to be able to connect with kids your age. If we do independent study, then you're only going to be more isolated."

"At least I'll be isolated from Terrence and Freddy."

"As nice as that may sound, Walter, isolation is not a realistic way to go through life."

Why not? Walter doesn't dare ask this but often wonders about it. *Why can't I be by myself? Read my books, do my work, and not get picked on—why isn't that an option?* This is once more on his brain as his mother calls him to the kitchen. She wants to talk about the zoo.

"Do you remember falling at the zoo last month?"

"Did they call again?"

"Yes, but they weren't checking on you this time."

"What did they want?"

"Do you remember telling them how you saw something under the concrete?"

"Yeah, a box."

"Remind me why you thought there was a box down there."

"I guess, when I fell, I sort of saw it."

"You mean you felt it? Like it was sticking up out of the ground?"

"No. I just—I closed my eyes, and I could tell it was there. I saw it."

"Like *X-Ray-vision* 'saw it'?"

"Mom!" Walter finds this comparison absurd. "When I fell, I think I put my hand down to stop myself. Then my hand kinda twitched, like moved, across the concrete." Walter waits for Elizabeth to interrupt. She does not, so he continues, "My eyes were shut, but there were a couple of little things I could see, and then I saw the whole box. It's happened before."

Elizabeth knows that hearing a kid explain even something simple can be an experience, so she carefully asks, "When did it happen before?"

"When I was looking for one of Annie's toys, the same thing happened. My hand moved, and then I saw the toy in my head."

"You could see where the toy was but not with your eyes?"

"Yeah. I found it in her toy pile, at the bottom, underneath everything else."

"But it wasn't underground or anything."

"Why would Annie's toys be underground?"

Elizabeth ignores. "The zoo called. They were redoing the sidewalk by where you fell. They found a box."

"Cool. What was in it?"

"Walter, I think you're missing the point. They found a box."

"I know. I told you they would."

"But I'm not getting how you knew that."

It is a scene from an old Western: two people on opposite sides of an understanding. Walter takes his best shot, "X-Ray vision?"

Seizing the opportunity his mother's hesitancy affords him, Walter returns upstairs to his siblings. Elizabeth is left with no clearer picture than before and still needs to relay the news to her son: the zoo found a time capsule in the box and wants Walter to do a TV interview later in the day.

***

It takes Walter 90 minutes to agree to do the interview. Elizabeth's case rests on that fundamental parenting truth: trying new things is good for you. Once Elizabeth can coax Walter through his initial anxiety and then its second stronger wave, she finally makes the bribe of a trip to Willie's Burgers. Walter is on board. News 10 is coming to the zoo to speak to him on camera alongside the zoo's director. Walter insists that his mom also stand next to him during the taping. Once Elizabeth's anxiety fades, she agrees and asks her sister over to help rehearse. Aunt Carol manages a downtown floral shop and promises to be by as soon as she finishes one last order for the day.

Maybe I'm mishearing him. Maybe what he's describing is perfectly normal. It'll probably make sense to Carol. She goes for these kinds of things.

The kids buzz in their aunt from the outdoor gate. She has brought a single red rose, which she hands with a bow to Walter at the front door, "For the star of the show."

"Aunt Carol, do I get anything?" Annie squawks from below.

"Oh, Annie, you get the best gift ever. You get to hang out with Mitch and me while your mom and brother go do boring stuff." There is enough enthusiasm in Carol's voice that she could sell Annie on anything. The little girl celebrates.

Elizabeth turns to her sister once the flower is in a vase. "Sis, you ready?"

"Let's do it." Carol looks at Walter. "Walt, you got your message points ready?"

"My what?"

"Message points. I heard someone at a business seminar say that one time. Sounded awful."

Walter and the adults walk up the townhome's slender staircase while Annie and Mitchell make a mild ruckus downstairs. The sisters sit on the bed in Elizabeth's room as Walter faces them from the door's threshold. Before any rehearsing can be done, Carol scans the room and interjects, "Okay, so my first note is that for a zoo, I was expecting a lot more animals." Elizabeth greets this comment with her traditional eye roll while Walter smiles and relaxes.

Elizabeth steers things back on course, "Walter, I'm going to pretend to be the interviewer. Your aunt will be the camera."

"How flattering," Carol quips.

"Young man, can you tell us about that day at the zoo last month?" Elizabeth is locked in.

"Okay, well, I was playing tag with my brother, which I know I'm not supposed to do. But my mom wasn't watching me so—"

"Cut," Elizabeth holds up her hand as Carol bursts out laughing. "Honey, I would really appreciate it if you could come up with a version of the story where I'm not a bad parent."

Walter smiles agreeably, "Okay." He collects himself. "I was running at the zoo when I tripped and fell. I landed with my hands on the ground."

"Sorry to hear that, young man. Were you hurt?"

"Mom, they are not going to ask that."

"They may to be nice."

Clearing his throat, Walter refocuses, "Not really. I wasn't hurt."

"And when you fell, you say you saw something? Can you tell me what you saw?"

"I saw a box."

"And can you tell us where this box was?"

"It was underground."

Carol shoots her sister a glance, which Elizabeth responds to with a confirming nod.

"And how did you see it if it was underground?"

Walter is more prepared than earlier. "You know how if you have deja vu, you think you see something twice. Except the first time only exists in your head. It was like that."

"You saw it in your head?"

"Yes." There is an extra pause in the room. Walter stands resolutely.

"Carol, do you have any questions for Walter?"

Carol gathers herself, "Mr. Crane, is it? First off, who does your hair? It's simply fabulous. Secondly, when you saw this so-called box, how could you be sure it really was there?"

"Well, it was there." Walter is alarmed by his aunt's sudden skepticism.

"I understand, but how were you sure it wasn't a daydream or a mistake or anything?"

"I don't know." Walter thinks. He hopes the actual TV interviewer does not ask this many questions. "Aunt Carol, you know how we watch *Jeopardy* sometimes?"

"The best times."

"And I will say an answer—"

"A question."

"A question. And it will be right. And maybe I didn't know I knew that fact ahead of time, but during the game, it somehow came to me? Like, I put together a name I knew with some part of the clue and guessed it. Well, it's like that. Like, it was in my memory, and I just had to find it."

Elizabeth is satisfied with the rehearsal. She dismisses Walter downstairs, "We'll get ready to leave in about thirty minutes." Walter exits, and then the two sisters wait until they no longer hear the creak of the hallway. When they are sure he is safely out of earshot, Elizabeth and Carol face each other like they are back to being kids again.

"How did his last doctor's visit go?" Carol is looking for a simple explanation.

"Fine. Nothing internally has ever worried them. And everything on the outside has been healed for a while."

"And no other changes?"

"No. He still reads a lot, still hates school. He *has* stopped coming to the room at night though."

"Oh?"

"He says I baby him."

"Well, he *is* getting older."

"How profound." Carol's sassiness has not taken long to rub off on her sister.

"And you're worried he's going to say all that during the interview?"

"I'm sure he's going to say all that during the interview."

"Well, maybe it's the truth. His truth, at least."

"Okay. But regardless of how he explains it, I'm still a little concerned about how it happened. Carol, he somehow managed to see a box buried under concrete."

"Aren't teachers always saying kids should learn one new skill over the summer?"

Elizabeth senses her sister is done being helpful, "Hilarious."

***

The simple interview turns into a live remote piece. Walter and Elizabeth are too preoccupied with the scorching 5 PM Sacramento sun to be bothered anymore by TV nerves. At the Crane household, Aunt Carol and Mitchell wade diligently through the lead stories, while Annie is less dedicated. National reports on political discontent and local reports on the homeless crisis test her patience. By the time her mom and brother make it on screen, she has invented a new dance and song, making it nearly impossible to pay attention to the interview.

The interview is brief. The zoo director steals much of the segment to tout the facility's upgrades. Walter answers three questions, including, yes, he was hurt but not much.

The last question gives him open court to parade his "vision" story for mass consumption. Elizabeth unknowingly grips his hand while he speaks, "I saw the box when I touched the ground. Sometimes I can see through things. I see through them in my head."

A voice in the interviewer's earpiece already indicated a need to wrap up before Walter began speaking; as a result, the interviewer is not paying close attention to his response. However, the zoo director looks at Walter how her employee did weeks ago, how Carol did earlier, and how Elizabeth has during all these times. The home audience mostly chalks the confusion up to "kid speak" or failing closed captions. In fact, of all the people who have heard Walter speak in person or on TV during the last month, the only one to be convinced is twenty-eight-year-old George Bates. He watches the interview with a look as though a mystery has been solved. He will tell his boss about it in the morning. A plan will be put in place.

Chapter 5

A black SUV waits at the corner across from Richfield Elementary. George Bates sits in the driver's seat with a baseball cap snug on his head. Exiting the car and closing the door sharply, George's twin sister, Jamie, wears dark designer sunglasses. As she reaches the school's dismissal area, she is flanked by parents, caretakers, and afterschool staff, who prepare for the bell's arrival at 3:07. Jamie spent the night before researching "what do moms wear" before ultimately opting for black yoga pants and a loose purple top. She also wears a pair of matching wedges and wonders how well she can run in them if it comes down to it.

In their late 20s, single, childless, and with little likelihood of a change in those circumstances, George and Jamie feel uncomfortable being so close to a school. This is not their element. The plan to take Walter, force him into the back of their car, and speed away— that's natural. That gives them no pause. For the past decade, they have committed various felonies on behalf of their employer.

While kidnapping has not been the cornerstone of their criminal careers, they have partaken occasionally. Their most recent such mark, about two years ago, was the wife of a wealthy philanthropist. Her husband possessed land and a passion for conservation that bewildered the Bates' boss. So George and Jamie took hold of the wife until ownership of 250 prime acres switched hands. The specifics of what was desired from this transaction were not of concern to the twins; their lack of curiosity may be their greatest occupational asset. George achieves relative moral satisfaction because violence is not a common stylistic choice of theirs. However, Jamie's feelings on the subject are more open to interpretation, as she hides inside her thoughts and behind those cat-eye frames.

It is the Thursday before Labor Day, the first day of school, so there is more commotion than usual. Three dozen parents stand outside the front gates anticipating the impending stampede of children. Meanwhile, Elizabeth Crane is in the middle of checking out books, movies, board games, and everything else her library offers. Too young for school, Annie hangs out with Aunt Carol at the flower shop, alternating between poking herself with thorns and almost eating rose petals. The plan is for Walter and Mitchell to walk home together and wait for the rest of the crew to join them later that evening.

Elizabeth has checked the time often today. It was a weird summer for the Cranes, especially as it was the first one as a single-parent family. Added to that abnormality were Walter's "mind tricks," as Elizabeth has begun calling them. However, the zoo, the field trip, her husband—none of that is given a thought now. She is too busy having a staring contest with the clock across the library's checkout desk and wondering if Walter is okay.

If dismissal is at 3:07, Elizabeth again tells herself, then Mitchell and Walter should be home by 3:22. At that point, Mitchell is to call from his cheap cellphone meant for emergencies and check-ins. The phone does not do anything "cool" like he wants, but that is not why he has it, Elizabeth continually reminds him.

***

Life has a way of solving one problem and then opening up another. It's that old cartoon bit where a finger is placed over a leak, only for another opening to arise, barely out of reach. School went well today. Walter saw Terrence and Freddy, but they were probably the only two that didn't look at him, as he was the talk of the recess yard following his burgeoning TV career. Walter was even asked for his autograph. Now, as he walks out of the gates to wait for his brother, he is gliding. Then the second leak presents itself. For the first time, the young boy hears the voice of Jamie Bates, "Walter."

Walter turns around, unsurprised. "Stranger danger" is not an immediate reflex. In the months since his father's passing, Walter has been picked up from school by an eclectic group of people: family, neighbors, and Elizabeth's coworkers. He assumes Jamie works at the library with his mother, so he walks to her obediently. Jamie is pleased with how easy this is so far. At least the rich guy's wife tried to run.

Jamie is the one who handles the leg work today, as a strange man amongst the waiting parents would have earned George at least one look of suspicion. Jamie does not have that problem. "Come with me," she plainly instructs as she places her hand on Walter's shoulder and guides him to the car. Even as she applies force to his back to steer him away, no one thinks twice about it except Walter. He tilts his head towards her, his eyebrows climbing his face to ask, "what's going on?" However, before he can say anything, he is on the sidewalk and then at the crosswalk. *Mitchell!* Walter sees his brother behind him in the distance.

Mitchell is casually glancing around the front of the school. On most days, he would be alarmed if Walter was not already waiting for him. *Trouble with bullies* would be a safe bet, but Mitchell saw how popular his little brother was today—*signing more autographs, probably*. With all the first-day excitement around him, Mitchell never spots Walter being pushed away.

George starts the engine when he sees his sister and the boy nearing. He thinks Walter looks even frailer than he did on the news segment that has brought them together. Walter is walking with minor resistance. His heavy backpack and Jamie's firm grip stifle any squirming, but Walter's real impediment is that he is not here right now. He is off again in his head, counting. A lifetime of turtling when events become tense has allowed him to avoid uncomfortable moments in the past, but this is not a moment that will go away and allow life to resume. This moment will change the shape of everything that follows. He needs to be here. Unfortunately, except for a soft yelp and a few neck-turns back in the direction of the school, Walter is not making Jamie work hard.

The SUV's driver-side rear seat door is popped open as Jamie marches Walter onward. The boy sees inside. The car's tinted windows and black interior create the effect of a dark hole, a path with no exit route. *Stop counting!* Walter knows where he is headed. The backseat is less than ten feet away. He's walking the plank. Five feet. Suddenly, he makes his shoulders go limp and shoots his arms down his sides. His backpack falls and clunks against the concrete. It does not produce enough sound to alert anyone, but it is enough of a disturbance to distract Jamie momentarily. Walter frees his shoulder and takes a single step away before her hand grabs his forearm and grasps tightly onto his wrist. She whips him back towards her and shoves him into the car, her wedges a minor nuisance. Jamie climbs in after Walter, forcing him to the passenger side as she directs her brother to "Go."

With no regard for the immediate stop sign, the SUV speeds off. The hiccup in the transfer has not alerted a soul. Jamie is pissed, and Walter has a sore wrist to complement his sore shoulder, but everything is progressing as intended. Mitchell keeps nonchalantly standing out front until five minutes have passed. He moves around to see if his brother is crouched down somewhere. The first few places he checks produce no positive results, so he heads to the corner. *Did Walter start walking home already?* As Mitchell chases this suspicion, he notices something familiar lying on the ground across the street: his brother's backpack.

Textbooks, binders, folders, pencil case, school-assigned book, pleasure-reading book, first-day packet, empty lunchbox, and a half-filled water bottle. Mitchell's investigation of Walter's backpack does not give him any clue as to his brother's whereabouts. With his thoughts now firmly on a Terrence-Freddy scenario, Mitchell slings the deserted pack over his shoulder, its weight at least twice that of his own.

Every alleyway Mitchell peers down is fruitless. Walter-flees-from-bullies has happened before, so he is not alarmed. However, Elizabeth is. It is now 3:30, and Mitchell senses his mom's panic as soon as he answers the phone. "Mitchell, why haven't you called?"

"I'm still walking."

"What happened?!" Elizabeth asks as though she is trying to clutch a corner of the world with one hand. She has already decided that something awful has occurred.

"I can't find Walter."

"What do you mean? Where is he?"

"Mom, I said I can't find him."

"Did you check the office?"

"They don't let kids in the office on the first day."

"Mitchell, did you check!" She's not asking anymore.

"I found his backpack."

"I don't understand. I thought you said you didn't know where he was."

"I don't. But I found his backpack across the street."

"Why would it be across the street?"

"I don't know. I was late walking out, so I went to the corner to see if he walked home already. But I only saw his backpack."

"You were late?"

"The teacher let us out late. It was only like two minutes. Walter knows to wait for me."

"I'm leaving work right now. Stay at school. I'll pick you up."

"I'm not at school anymore."

"You're home already?"

"I will be in a couple blocks."

"Mitchell, what if your brother is back at school waiting for you? He doesn't have a way to call you. Only you have the phone. That's why you're supposed to stick together." As she talks, Elizabeth stops pacing around the break room, retrieves her purse, and considers who can cover the rest of her shift.

Mitchell pauses. He is unsure how to talk to his mom or rationalize any part of whatever seems to be taking place right now. "Mom, I'm trying. If Walter was still at school, he would've been smart enough to ask someone to call. I think he ran off because Terrence and Freddy were chasing him."

"You saw them chase him?" Elizabeth interrupts herself when she finds Manuel, a recent divorcee eager to take on more hours. Mitchell has responded to his mother's question, but she is not listening. "Manny, I have a thing with Walter. Can you cover me?"

Manny answers, "of course," with a smile that temporarily alleviates a portion of Elizabeth's worry.

"Thanks." Elizabeth rushes out of the room as the tightness returns to her jaw. She then returns to the phone, "Mitchell, how close to home are you?"

"Almost there."

"Okay, when you get there, stay there. Keep your ringer on loud. I'm going to the school. Then—" *Then I'm going to come home with Walter, and we'll all be fine again.* "I'll see you when I get home."

***

Fifty minutes pass. Mitchell is waiting for his mom, for his brother, anyone. Annie is still with Aunt Carol, he assumes. Being home by himself is typically more fun than this. He makes a peanut butter and jelly sandwich and watches YouTube. After an hour, the front door opens. Elizabeth walks in alone. She haphazardly places her keys and purse on the living room dresser and then sits on the edge of the sectional couch opposite Mitchell. Mitchell pauses his video and crumples his napkin as he waits to hear what his mom knows:

1. Walter walked off school grounds with a woman. It was crowded, and the school's security footage is grainy, but Walter didn't run from her.
2. The video didn't capture much aside from Walter and the woman's initial steps from the school. During this time, they both had their backs to the camera. Walter never turned around or pulled away.
3. No neighbors reported seeing anything out of the ordinary. Several said they typically turn up the

volume on their TVs when school gets out. No one has home cameras.

4. The school will make an all-call tonight. The police have opened a missing person case.

That is all Elizabeth can say right now. She wants to cuss, scream, and cry, but she does not want to scare Mitchell. She wants to cuss and scream a little at him, but she knows it is not his fault. If he had been out on time, maybe two of her kids would be missing now.

My kid is missing.

Unsure how to process the moment, Elizabeth leaves Mitchell without an extra word. This is the first first day of school where she has not bombarded him with questions, and he misses it. After trudging upstairs to her bedroom, Elizabeth shuts the door and collapses onto the bed. Then the tears come.

There is a frightening place inside a parent's mind. It is absent of light but filled with silence. It is where mothers and fathers go to contemplate the worst possible. This place has no discernible visuals because you fight to keep images away. Seeing something concrete only serves to make it seem real. Elizabeth reminds herself that despite the part of her brain asking what if something horrific has happened, she should be thinking about what if Walter is safe and everything soon to be restored to whatever passes for normal these days.

Elizabeth was in therapy in her adolescence and early adulthood. Believing the worst was most likely was the product of schoolyard anxiety that never let up. While no incidents left outward marks of trauma, Elizabeth kept that tension inside her like the filling of a tooth, metallic and piercing if encountered the wrong way. She would find healthy methods to manage it in her 20s, empowered with coping skills and a supportive partner. The anxiety flared up occasionally when Mitchell was born, but he hit all his milestones on time. He never had that high fever that wouldn't break or that fall that made them gasp. Elizabeth's life was in sync.

Mitchell was the kind of child who convinces you that parenthood is simple, whereas Walter proved how challenging it could be. A deep-seated pessimism that Elizabeth had tried to deny came roaring back as a struggle took shape between good and bad days. Annie was, in part, an attempt to overthrow the stress that had seized her with Walter, to recover her balance. And Annie, though wild and reckless, has delivered precisely that. However, when Elizabeth isolates her thoughts on Walter and senses the weakness in him that others seem to prey on, she is lost again. Her husband died, and all three of her children are scarred because of it, but there are moments when she feels that this loss will be imprinted more on Walter. It is not that her parenting is insufficient or some lie about a boy requiring a dad. No, Walter needs allies. He is a vulnerable kid who may carry that vulnerability throughout his years. Walter's dad had been a protector. Right now, Walter has none.

This is the thought pressing down on top of Elizabeth. This is the dark place she knows she must avoid, even as she is drawn towards it. Under her eyes, tears pool together; some escape and trickle down her cheek. Elizabeth is in a slow, aching cry. Then the doorbell rings. She bolts up in bed and checks her phone. No calls or messages. After wiping under each eye twice with a shirt sleeve, she hears Mitchell open the door and Annie's voice trumpet through the house. Elizabeth races out of the room and down the stairs to give them the biggest hugs they have ever had.

Chapter 6

Walter sleeps on a cot. A plain blue blanket drapes over him in a windowless room—the blanket so new the sales tag has yet to be removed. On the car ride over, Walter alternated between tears and mumbled refrains of, "Oh, God." These repeated utterances eventually wore on Jamie, so she turned the car stereo up, hoping it would silence the crying. George drove on, knowing better than to power-struggle with his sister over something as trivial as the radio.

As he was too distracted in the car to track its movements, Walter finally realized they were where they were meant to be when the vehicle eased into an underground garage. Jamie, no longer worried that someone might question her hands on the boy, grabbed his wrist tightly as she yanked him from the car, across the garage, and into the narrow room now acting as his home. The room is covered in aluminum fencing, and in one corner, an industrial-sized water heater shrills with the occasional metallic ping. Neither of the twins is watching their housemate too closely. Following a whispered conversation about food, George gets up and leaves.

Jamie is the older sibling, technically only by 18 minutes, but people are often surprised that she and George are even related. Her life goal is to save enough money and move to a house with a fireplace and no neighbors. Her job is a means to that end, a clever route to cash without the false niceties required in other lines of employment. While operating alongside her brother poses issues, Jamie does not have to pretend with him. Their relationship is primarily a working one: George handles the customer service side of things, while Jamie tends to janitorial concerns. They complement each other well, despite their understandings not always being mutual.

As Jamie looks at a dozing Walter, she does not see some pathetic boy needing help or even a pesty, snot-ridden pre-teen. She sees an object, a parcel, something she was assigned to acquire and ensure can perform specific tasks in the coming week. After observing him long enough to see that he's breathing regularly, Jamie swivels her chair to a laptop computer. She is custom-designing a pair of sunglasses. This is her happy place.

George returns later with two brown fast food bags and one plastic bag of groceries, mostly trail mix and bananas. As the twins eat, the smell of food and the sound of their chewing wakes Walter. He arises, expecting to find the recognizable shadows cast by his blinds back home; instead, there is only the cold uncertainty of his new living space. The younger Bates is the first to notice Walter waking. He motions to his sister with a nod and then to Walter with a point of a half-eaten hamburger. A disinterested Jamie stays with her food, but her brother walks over with a cup of soda to offer the boy a drink. Walter sits up and takes a few sips from the plastic straw, blinking away the remaining cobwebs.

"Where am I?"

"You're safe."

"What are you doing with me?"

"We're going to be watching you for a while."

"Watching me do what?"

"Kid, don't worry. You'll be fine."

The banter begins to irk Jamie. "George, stop. Give him his food and stop."

George brings over a chicken sandwich and what's left of a container of fries. He places them next to the soda he dropped off earlier. A minute goes by before Walter carefully interrupts their chewing with another line of questions."Is your name 'George'? Why are you doing this?" George is not necessarily surprised that Walter has used his name but is unsure how to respond. When Walter is met with silence, he meekly offers up again, "George—"

Jamie cuts in, "Walter Crane. 1114 Coach Street. Your mom's name is Elizabeth. She works at the Central

Library. You have a younger sister, Anne, and an older brother, Mitchell. That information doesn't give me power. That I'm bigger and stronger than you gives me power." No one is eating anymore. "You know George's name. I let you know that. We didn't blindfold you on the way in. We're not wearing masks. Knowing whatever you know doesn't matter if you have no one to tell it to." Jamie never raises her voice. She does not have to.

Turning over in his bed, Walter has his back to the twins. He is too sad to be hungry, too tired to break down, too scared to ask more questions, and too confused to solve his way out. The set-up reminds Walter of his hospital room, where nurses came in and out to check his IV. He is here, and other people are here, but there is a disconnect between them. Abruptly, Walter sees Jamie leave, followed soon after by the sound of a cellphone buzzing. A brief call features George mostly speaking in "yes" responses. At one turn in the talk, George states, "He's fine.... You know what I mean." Walter tosses this statement around, but George hangs up and approaches before he can crack its meaning.

"You should eat." No response. "Well, your food is going to get soggy if it isn't already, but you should eat. You're going to need the energy for tomorrow." No response. "I'm taking the laptop with me. These walls are thick concrete. There's no phone line. If you have to pee, there's a bucket in the corner. I'm sorry, but that's all there is for now." Suddenly, Walter has to go to the bathroom but then looks at the bucket and decides against it.

"Why are you doing this?"

George pauses and then answers, "Like I said, kid, eat something." Before Walter can officially register another non-response, George leaves, locking the door from the outside. Once Walter is sure that his second captor is away, he throws his legs over the side of the bed and stands up. It is the first time he has stood on his own since being forced off school grounds earlier. Every inch of him alarms with disorientation.

Walter confirms that the door is locked. When he bangs on it with a fist, the door answers hopelessly. He wants to improvise a weapon or communication device to get an advantage over George and Jamie, but not much is around; instead, Walter returns to his cot and his as-promised withered food. The tarnished corner of an overhead fluorescent light fixture has his attention. He stares at it as he nibbles on a soggy fry. Walter is convinced that this is the worst first day of school ever.

***

"He just walked with her." Elizabeth's earlier disbelief has given way to something more fatalistic. She is upstairs theorizing with Carol. "He saw her. He walked over to her and walked off with her. That's it."

"Sis, stop talking like that. Maybe he thought she was someone's mom, a classmate's."

Elizabeth dismisses this suggestion about her friendless son with her eyebrows pulled in tight. "Why didn't he run?" There is no correct answer. There is nothing that Elizabeth will hear that will allow her not to beat herself up. The moment's shock has burned off and been replaced by a storm of self-doubt.

Carol has to be the grounded one now. "What reason does Walter have to run away? What single instance of not returning your love have you ever witnessed? So he expressed some . . . *dissatisfaction* recently, but what's that? That's normal for his age." Elizabeth is not buying it, but Carol presses on, "Look, Annie and Mitchell need you. I bet they're as scared as you are—well, probably not Annie. Anyway, how 'bout I go walk the neighborhood and ask around, and you go downstairs with them?"

After a brief pause, Elizabeth concedes, "You're right."

"Of course, I'm right. And I'm sure this will all be settled by the time you go to bed."

Minutes later, Carol steps outside the Crane residence and exhales. Of all the things she told her sister, the promise of a swift resolution is the one she has difficulty believing. When Carol considers Walter alone, she cannot envision him experiencing sudden success in that arrangement. He has spent most of kiddom tied to his mother—so *where does that leave him now?*

***

Downtown Sacramento is a grid marked with numbers and letters. Around quitting time, you mostly find state workers who want to get home without committing themselves to a new conversation.

"Excuse me, have you seen this boy?" Carol holds up her cellphone. A picture of Walter from this past summer, clad in a tank top and swim shorts, is displayed. Most people politely say "'no'" or shake their heads to the same effect. Some walk by with headphones in their ears; others take phone calls that happen to last precisely as long as they are in Carol's immediate vicinity.

"Is he lost?"

"He didn't come home from school today... No, he doesn't have a phone. Yes, the police have been contacted. No, he doesn't have any friends or relatives in the area."

Carol stands in front of the State Capitol's west steps. From its perch atop the nearby Tower Bridge, the sun bakes the government building's white façade. After a failed survey of the south side, Carol is set to continue her loop when she spies a swarm of tourists, cameras ready. Reflexively, she retreats. She is not mentally prepared to play photographer, so she heads towards the sun, down Capitol Mall, stopping at bus stops and crosswalks, hoping for a miracle. The Capitol is shrinking in the background, and the Cranes are now a good twenty minutes in her rearview. As Carol considers turning around, she has an epiphany, "He's in Old Sac!" A state worker strolling ahead of Carol hears this remark and jerks her head back. Carol submissively nods but keeps walking. If Walter had to choose one place to visit, it would be Old Sacramento. Its built-in history and candy stores are tailor-made for her lovable nerd, sugar addict of a nephew. The kidnapping theory is preposterous to Carol. She finds it far more believable that Walter consented to run errands with a friend's mom and is now being rewarded with taffy from Candy Heaven. *Elizabeth didn't recognize the woman in the video because the picture quality was poor. Or the woman had a haircut. Or Elizabeth is being forgetful.*

In the five minutes it takes Carol to move from the scene of her revelation to the heart of Old Sacramento, her enthusiasm tempers, but she remains hopeful. However, after searching up and down the neighborhood's rickety cross boards and cobblestone streets, that hope begins to dim. Carol asks travelers and locals, even the homeless, who find refuge in Old Sac's alleyways. Nothing productive. A sweatshirted man in a duct-taped wheelchair admits he cannot help but wishes her "a blessed day." Carol makes stops at Walter's favorite stores. The "haven't seen him" responses are kinder than she was getting before but still unpromising. Finally, she arrives at the outskirts of Old

Sacramento. Across from her sits a retired four-deck riverboat, the Delta King. The boat is most recognized for its red sternwheel but offers no reward today. No one has seen Walter. Many suggest calling the cops; others do the fake phone maneuver.

Carol takes a pensive last look at the river and recalls that it stretches for hundreds of miles. She worries that her "Walter is with a friend" idea does not have legs. A disappointed text is sent to Elizabeth, and Elizabeth replies similarly. As Carol returns to the Capitol, the sun on her back, questions swirl: *why*, *how*, and *who?* Unknowingly, she is on the edge of an answer to her latter query. Just outside the Capitol's underground parking entrance, she crosses paths with a twenty-something short-haired woman in designer glasses. Jamie Bates is exiting the armed-off driveway when Carol attempts to get her attention, "Excuse me, have you—"

Moving with swift strides, Jamie speeds out of the way. Carol has been ignored plenty today, but this woman didn't even have headphones or the decency to pretend to take a call. Tired from her failed mission, Carol's default fun, free-spirited state is compromised. She mutters under her breath and gives Jamie an annoyed second look. Hers is a face Carol will remember.

Chapter 7

It is Friday morning. A lone ant scavenges on the floor beneath Walter's cot. Its splayed limbs awkwardly climb the metal legs supporting the boy's restless sleep. Soon it finds warmth in the curve of his neck, his skin tense and dotted with clusters of light freckles. Walter adjusts in response to the ant's arrival while the ant stays the course and continues up his chin. This time, Walter sends his hand to nudge the insect intruder away, flicking it back to the floor. The ant scurries off as the boy slowly opens his eyes. He sees George and Jamie standing over him and jumps to consciousness. It feels like they have been watching him forever and like he has been away from his family for twice as long.

"You're awake." Upon hearing George's voice, Walter is horrified to learn that yesterday was real. He sits up and stares. The twins stare back. "You can have a banana for breakfast," George informs.

"And then we have some work to do." Jamie's voice possesses a detachment that erases any influence of context.

She could be in the middle of a storm or on a tropical beach, and her voice would sound the same.

Some work. Walter is disturbed by the vagueness of those two words. It takes him five minutes to accept a morning dose of potassium and then one more to discover what "some work" means.

There is a metal box, a foot long and half as tall. Its depth lies between those two measurements, and a silver lock lies on top. George carries the box by its leather handle and sets it at the end of Walter's cot. Jamie never moves but looks at Walter as if he instantly knows what to do with an industrial-grade security box. He does not.

"Tell us what's in the box." Jamie is finished implying, but the boy's eyes, pulsing with bewilderment, only offer two large vacancy signs. She is not used to being looked at so absently. "Tell us what's in the box," Jamie repeats, figuring it was a mere issue of articulation that has led to Walter's dumbfounded state.

"How do I—I don't know what's in the box. What's in the box? How would I know what's in the box?" Each time Walter says "box," he increases his level of franticness.

Jamie looks over at her brother, "Kuda Bux."

Walter's head begins to throb. He's not even sure if Jamie is saying actual words anymore. "Walter," George tries to translate. "Walter, do your thing, tell us what's in the box." A day removed from the familiar, Walter has already lost connection to his name.

"Thing? I don't have a thing."

"Your TV thing. You can see through stuff, right?"

"I don't have a thing."

"Goddamned liar!" Jamie makes "liar" sound like a marathon of flames.

George tries a softer, closer approach, "Kid, all we want you to do is tell us what's in the box. You were on TV, right?"

Walter nods.

"At the zoo, you could tell what was under the concrete, right?"

Walter nods.

"You saw what was there without looking at it, right?"

Walter nods.

"So, how'd you do it?" Walter does not nod, so George proceeds, "On the news, you said you fell. Your face must have hit the ground. Do you need to put your face next to the box? Whatever you need," George is revealing a trace of desperation. "We only want you to tell us what's inside."

Walter fixates on the box. *Can Superman see through metal? Why hasn't Mom found me?* He settles on, "Can I have some water?" Jamie sighs angrily and walks away. George and Walter both think she is going to grab one of the plastic bottles of water sitting on the workstation across the room; instead, Jamie takes a seat and glares at the wall. Walter is happy she is gone but still thirsty. Mercifully, George retrieves a bottle, and Walter takes a big gulp. He hands the drink back to George.

"I don't control it. It just happened."

"Kuda Bux," Jamie murmurs dismissively.

"What is she saying?"

"Excuse my sister. She's a bit cynical at times. She said, 'Kuda Bux.' Ever heard of him?" Walter has not. "He was this old magician. From Pakistan. You know where that is? It's in the Middle East."

"I know where Pakistan is." The water helped, but George's newly relaxed tone is also responsible for Walter calming down enough to process the moment.

"Right, well, he was this magician, a firewalker, a bunch of things." George first encountered Kuda Bux in a sophomore-year English class. School had long been a six-hour struggle to pay attention, but George found himself mellowing out in his teens and encountering a few lessons that caught his interest. Kuda Bux's ability to adapt to circumstances through sheer willpower was particularly inspiring. "His best performance had to do with a blindfold. He would get doctors to put on surgical tape—the stuff they use in hospitals—all around his eyes. Then he could read words, hit targets, all sorts of things, and all while blindfolded." As George becomes more animated in his description, Jamie's sneers grow in volume. "When we heard you talk about the zoo, it sounded the same."

"But I wasn't blindfolded."

"And we're not asking you to be. Kuda Bux could only see things that other people already saw. You're different. You can see what no one else knows exists. The point is people are capable of more than what we give them credit for. *Skeptics*. You know that word?" Walter nods, leaving George encouraged. "Well, there were some that called Kuda Bux a fraud, who said there must be a trick to how he walked on fire or read while blindfolded. But if you think about it—there are billions of people alive today. As far as people who have ever lived, like 100 billion, a hella big number. I don't know about you, but when I think about all those people, I imagine that within those billions, there must be a few who can do things the rest of us can only imagine. *Kuda Bux*."

Maybe George is a middle school history teacher or a motivational sports coach in another life. However, in this life, he is a career criminal in the middle of a kidnapping, trying to convince his victim about the merits of a Middle Eastern mystic. At least Walter is buying it, but now he feels like he is letting George down, "I understand, but I can't. I did see under the ground, but I don't know how. I'm sorry. I can't control it."

"Okay, but will you try? Walter, for me? Have another sip, concentrate, and try."

George hands the drink back to Walter, and the boy takes a dramatic swallow, followed by a smooth, soothing breath. He edges near the box and inspects it, hoping some vision will pop into his head, and then George and Jamie will let him go back to his family, and that will be that. Walter places his fingertips on the box's front. *Nothing.* He moves his hand to the top, setting his palm against the keyhole. It is cool to the touch as he leaves it there. *Nothing*. After scooching back along the bed, Walter faces George with regret.

Jamie punctures the silence, "I knew it."

"It's okay, kid. Was the zoo the first time you did it?"

"There was one other time. With my sister."

"What did you find?"

"A toy."

"She had a toy underground?"

"Not really. It was in a pile of toys."

"I don't understand."

"I sort of placed my hand on top of the toys and then could see where the lost one was buried."

"You mean you saw it with your eyes?"

"No, in my head."

Finding a child's plaything in some family's living room is not bolstering George's confidence. "Okay, can you think about those two times? With your sister and the zoo—did they have anything in common?"

Walter is stumped. He fell at the zoo but was sitting in the living room with his sister. The toy was above ground. The capsule was underground. As Walter compares and contrasts, Jamie gets up with enough force that it pushes the chair to the back of the room, crashing into the protective fencing. She is not stopped by the collision's sound and walks to Walter with fury in her eyes. "He's worthless! He can't even see what's in a little box, so how is he going to help us! Huh! How is he going to help us, George!" The room's walls are so dense that they trap the violence in Jamie's voice. "This is your dumbass idea. I'm always the one who cleans up, but not this time!" Turning towards Walter, she crouches down and opens up, "Worthless! You weak, worthless little boy!" With the punctuation of "worthless," Walter's breath moves at a sprinter's pace. He tries counting, but the twins' yelling is challenging his escape.

1 . . .

"Jamie, stop!"

. . . 2

"You're so naive!"

. . . 3

"Give him a chance!"

. . . 4

"To do what? Fail again?"

. . . 5

Walter's short breaths ache in his chest. He places his hand back on top of the box to steady himself.

"You're such a . . ."

"I'm such a what?! Say it, George!" George does not answer, so Jamie continues, "What am I? Tell me. You're a goddamn coward! But tell me what I am!"

"It's a watch," Walter interrupts.

The plug is pulled, and the room falls still. George and Jamie stare at Walter. George looks back at his sister, suspended in rage. Walter looks at George for a hand as the younger Bates pulls a shiny key from his shirt pocket. He leans over the box, unlocks it, and throws open the lid.

Python-stamped leather. Silver dial. Yellow gold. *It's a watch.*

Chapter 8

Stone Archer sits behind a third-generation mahogany desk. Despite his grand view of the city, his blinds are drawn. Slits of sunlight fall across the leaves of a potted snake plant, while a single banker's lamp provides the only other source of illumination. Stone twirls a fountain pen in one hand as his other hand turns over page after page of California Senate bill proposals. His eyebrows are perfectly straight, except for a sudden incline lasting a few centimeters near their graying ends. The tedium of the government has long taken its toll. Stone figures that there are only two or three meaningful sentences among the thousands of words in front of him. His job is to find those key passages, bend them in his direction, and be out the door and across town for drinks no later than 4:00 PM.

Being president of the state senate is a job that affords Stone a respected title, a healthy salary, and a significant source of power. Following his rise to the upper ranks of the state government in the mid-2000s, he briefly considered national politics. However, meetings with kingmakers at the federal level left Stone to realize it would be another decade's climb to the upper ranks of Washington DC. After scraping through graduate school, the local scene in Fresno, and the back hallways of the state Capitol, Stone decided he was done going uphill. He has spent the rest of his time expanding outwards and now makes most of his income from sources beyond his elected position. A successful businessman does not often have his back to the wall. A successful politician does not even know walls exist.

They say Sacramento is amid a major redevelopment. They say Sacramento is poised to be America's next great big city. However, they won't admit that only a handful of marketable blocks are being renovated, primarily to accommodate the influx of Bay Area expatriates. Stone has been a central figure behind these changes, starting with relocating the city's professional sports team to the heart of downtown and pushing out any residents not rich enough to afford courtside seats. Lately, he has been pulling hard to snatch up land near the waterfront in Old Sacramento. For decades, this area has been seen as a novelty, a tourist trap, a place for school children to visit. Stone imagines it transformed into luxury apartments, high-end boutiques, and ritzy law offices. To date, his attempts to negotiate with its current owners have been insufficient, as have his attempts to get the city to condemn buildings or overturn the historical designation of others. Two years ago, Stone acquired 250 acres of nearby real estate but has yet to move on that land with any purpose. Every time he goes to Old Sac to imagine what could be, he is interrupted by stores peddling tacky trinkets, out-of-towners with their guts out, and the homeless in his way. On these days, he starts drinking earlier than 4:00.

Nine years ago, Stone met George Bates during a reelection campaign. He was cutting the ribbon at a troubled youth facility in Fresno when his eye for spotting talent led him to the young Mr. Bates. Stone saw a vitality that he envied in George and a willingness to do what others shied away from. His recruit was quickly given a job canvassing door-to-door in the rougher neighborhoods. After performing well in this role and showing an eagerness to do more work, Stone brought George to Sacramento. When George later informed his boss that he had a twin sister as discreet and even less scrupulous, the tenured politician smiled.

Stone has always looked at George as a long-term project: rough but full of potential. Six months back, after reading a *Sacramento Bee* article about an 1800s legend of lost gold, George brought the idea of buying the land to Stone. While he was proud of his pupil's enterprising ways, he told him that county permits, local protests, and environmental handwringers would likely hold up any exploration for years. He applauded the effort, George hung his head, and Jamie smirked at her little brother's ambition. Then Walter came into their lives.

What if we can know for sure where the gold is? We can keep the operation small, buy off any trouble, and be in and out before county officials give us a second look.

While not 100% sold on the logistics, Stone trusts the twins, especially Jamie. Should things go south, he knows she can clean up a mess. It's a win-win. If gold is gathered, he adds to his fortune. If nothing is found, he has empowered his underlings, who ultimately failed but now are further indebted to him. There is a difference, Stone knows, between being rich and being wealthy. The difference is power. Once he figured this out, he never looked back.

When Stone talks, his voice possesses a pleasant old-time radio quality. This Friday morning, he addresses a crowd of reporters outside city hall. His suit fits him well, not flashy but expertly tailored. He is known for crossing his arms when speaking, and this morning is no different. "The homeless in California have been ignored for too long. Today we put a stop to that. These men and women are veterans, mothers, fathers, sons, and daughters. They are struggling and in need of help. As a state, we have an obligation to all our citizens. We gather here today to see that obligation through." It is a surprisingly people-first address for a politician known more for crafting corporate tax loopholes.

"I have reached out to organizations throughout the state to craft a ten-point plan." The outline of his proposal—his *bipartisan* proposal, he is sure to mention—includes putting an end to citations for the homeless along the state's public trails and waterways and dedicating up to one billion dollars in funding for shelters. Locations for these shelters are still to be negotiated city by city, but, Stone notes, Sacramento will lead the way with a site along the river in the town's historic district.

The morning's announcement is met with dutiful applause. After all, no one wants to be publicly against housing for the homeless, but many wonder why Stone chose to be the face of this project. A big business politician suddenly making himself an activist for the unhoused is undoubtedly a left turn. Jokes about Ebenezer Scrooge are batted around, but Stone is too strong, and the issue is too explosive for anyone to be the first to speak out. He exits the platform with a practiced smile as TV reporters summarize his speech for upcoming broadcasts.

A gigantic all-black beast on wheels picks Stone up after his press conference. Excited staff members greet him with compliments, which he casually ignores. He knows that words to a politician often come with strings attached, just as words from a politician often hide a bundle. The homeless do not vote or donate to his campaign, so his care for their plight is all theater. His real concerns lie in verifying Walter's gifts and counting down the time until the Old Sacramento Business Association freaks out about his plan and comes running to make a deal.

***

After a long night of phone calls, social media posting, and little sleep, Elizabeth's alarm awakens her to day two of the unbelievable. It is eerily similar to when she woke up for the first time without her husband. Walter was never a loud kid, but the house is too quiet this morning. The absence of a loved one outweighs all.

Elizabeth isn't planning on working today, so she feels guilty about sending Mitchell to school. She debated the idea with her sister before they both decided that trying to give him some semblance of normality might be helpful. While more clued into what's going on than Annie, Mitchell still possesses that magical feeling of youth that things automatically work out. When his father died, he had a line of questions: "Is heaven real?"; "Can Dad still see me?"; "Can I talk to him?" However, after an initial interest in the subject, Mitchell seemed to shape back to his regular easy-going self, leaving Elizabeth to wonder how much he is hiding under the surface. While Walter shows his emotions like flashing neon, Mitchell's poker face is strong. Ultimately, struggles with grief and the practicality of single-parenthood have not permitted her to check in more frequently with her eldest. She regrets this, but now as she worries that her rawness over Walter may frighten Mitchell more, she decides to push these concerns further out of sight.

Annie and Mitchell talk endlessly on the walk to school. Their energy and volume levels are both running high, while Elizabeth feels like she is in two different places. She is going through the motions of motherhood: holding hands, serving reminders to look both ways, and answering questions about bugs, cars, and other random objects they pass. At the same time, she is removed from herself, from the walk, from the two kids, trying somehow to put herself with Walter. This juggling of competing headspaces presents a kind of parental disorientation, a sharper, more formidable anxiety than she has encountered before.

Mitchell is years beyond allowing his mom to hug him at school, so this morning, she compensates by squeezing Annie's hand and staring at her budding sixth-grader longer than usual as he runs in through the front gates. *Is this a mistake?* She considers going into the office to see if they have heard anything, but something stops her from taking a step further. As she looks to her left, where grainy video captured a life-altering incident less than 24 hours ago, Elizabeth realizes she wants no more part of this moment.

The distance from Richfield to the library is fifteen minutes walking. While Elizabeth has already texted her supervisor to say she is not up for work today, she still wants to go in for a couple of hours before opening to use the employee databases. At exactly the halfway point of their journey, Annie informs her mom that she has to go to the bathroom. Elizabeth breaks out of her distracted state as they race to the library. No accidents are had.

Mother and daughter walk down to the five-story building's lower level so Annie can play in the kid's area while Elizabeth follows up on a few curiosities. She will spend the next ninety minutes alternating between search engines, newspaper archives, public records databases, online forums, and most-wanted lists.

"my son is missing"
"how to find missing son"
"how to find missing child"
"find missing person" "tips"
"missing persons" "resources"
"Walter Crane"
"Walter Crane" "Sacramento"
"Sacramento kidnapping"
"Sacramento crime"
"95814 crime"
"known kidnappers"
"known kidnappers" "Sacramento"
"kidnapping prison sentence"
"missing child database"

"register missing child"

Elizabeth cannot help herself. She learned early on in her parenting that you do not Google your children's symptoms. A heat rash can turn into a deadly disease with a single click, but here she is, ignoring her better judgment, knocked over by the sheer number of missing children cases. Their names, where they are missing from, and when they went missing—it's all here. Next to this information is an image of each child, sometimes a smiling vacation picture, sand in the background, or a school portrait, hair done and collars tight with starch. A few photographs feature the children in sports gear, maybe the last soccer game they ever played. Elizabeth is entering that unhealthy place. Results are filtered state by state. Some of these children went missing the previous week, but she has never heard their stories. Some of these children went missing from Sacramento, but this is the first she has learned about them. Through clouded eyes, Elizabeth closes her browser, looks at Annie playing with the library's felt garden toys, and then reopens the internet.

"missing child support group"

Selecting a website entitled "Family Survival Guide," Elizabeth notices she has already fallen into the major traps:

not sleeping, keeping emotions bottled up, and blaming herself. The guide emphasizes a need to balance the dramatic shifts from hope to despair. Elizabeth agrees this is important but is not sure if it is realistic. Scrolling down, she finds "planning for the long-term," which forces her to wince and close the browser a final time.

Elizabeth fears thinking too far ahead. Looking at the individual trees is manageable because she knows immediately what a tree is and how a tree feels. There is control in the close-up. If she zooms out and sees the forest, the road leading in, and the hills in the distance, she's forced to process the entire scene and contemplate that some things may be beyond her grasp. For the time being, she will choose to see only the trees.

When the two arrive home, an exhausted Annie requests TV. With old cartoons blaring in the background, Elizabeth heads to the kitchen to rinse dishes left over from breakfast. One less bowl than usual. After loading the dishwasher, she returns to the living room to stare at her phone while Annie watches *Looney Tunes*. Elizabeth sends a "no news" text to her sister, a "checking in" text to Mitchell, and then a "checking in to see if there's any news" email to the officer in the Missing Persons Unit assigned to Walter's case. She hits send and then refreshes her inbox half a dozen times. Elizabeth senses herself slipping back into despair, so she tosses her phone aside and joins her daughter for some mindless television.

Wile E. Coyote is after the Road Runner. It is the same as when she was a kid. There is comfort in that. Wile schemes and chases and then runs off a cliff. He is magically floating in mid-air, poised over nothing but the hard ground below. After hovering in open space for a second, he makes the mistake of looking down. Elizabeth excuses herself to her bedroom.

Chapter 9

Walter wears a change of clothes paid for in cash at a downtown discount store. The new clothes mark a new day but one once more in captivity. Today, at least, offers a change in scenery as the boy sits in the backseat of the Bates' SUV, watching the familiarity of the city fade behind him. In the front, Jamie drives while George rides shotgun. Walter spends the trip to the Sacramento foothills gazing longingly out the car window, only breaking his concentration to play 21 questions with George.

"Where are we going?"

"Someplace where you can put your talent to good use."

"I told you I don't know how to control it."

"It didn't seem like you had trouble earlier."

"But I don't know how I did that."

"Well, we'll try until you see something."

"What if I don't see anything?"

"Let's not worry about that now."

"What happens if I don't see anything?"

"It would be disappointing."

"But what happens?"

"Honestly, kid, it doesn't matter. Plan B, I guess."

"What's Plan B?"

"We'll get to that if we have to."

"Can you at least tell me where we're going?"

George responds with a tired sigh, "The hills."

"What hills?"

"You know you ask a lot of questions."

"What hills?"

"Anyone ever told you that: you ask a lot of questions?"

"What hills?"

"The foothills."

"What's there?"

Jamie scrunches her forehead out of a growing annoyance, but George chuckles and takes a breath, "If I tell you what we're looking for, you're going to ask more questions. And if I answer those questions, you're probably going to ask some more. And it will only be once we get to where we're going that you're going to stop asking. So how about we both save ourselves the trouble and wait until we get there."

A hush in the car seems to indicate that Walter has agreed to this arrangement. Ten seconds pass. "What if you were me?"

George turns around, mildly interested, "What?"

"I don't know what's going on. I don't know who you are or what you want with me. I don't know where my family is or how they're doing. I don't know how long this is going to take. I'm in the back of a car with strangers going someplace to do something that I don't even know if I can. Just tell me where we're going and what I'm supposed to see. I'll shut up. I promise."

George moves his eyes to ask Jamie, but she wants no part of any proposed bargaining. *The kid makes sense, even if he is irritating.* "Walter, you're smart, so I'm guessing you've heard of the Gold Rush. We're going to where they found a lot of that gold, and you're going to tell us where we should be digging. Simple."

While he did not take a vow of immediate silence, Walter considers the crowd of questions filling his head. He decides to err on the side of caution, "Okay." George smiles and turns back around.

The rest of the ride features no talking, only the sound of the car going over increasingly older roads until they arrive at their destination. To the side of the highway is a collection of rocks and dirt slightly more significant than what might be called a patch. Jamie slows the car down until it rests on the far side of the makeshift lot. Walter had been looking for signs, towns, anything identifiable but found none, so the turn into gravel catches him by surprise. There are no other cars parked and only hills, faded green and shades of brown, to his right.

The foothills of Sacramento lie outside the city limits but within the expansive county boundaries. Gold was discovered here over 170 years ago. While only a few found the area profitable, this land was last explored with enthusiasm during a different technological time. Further swelling his anticipation, George is sure he has at his disposal something no miner or excavation company ever had: Walter.

After walking several hundred yards from the car, Walter notices no one in the group has any mining equipment. No shovels, no drills, no gadgets of any kind. In fact, the twins' only tools are completely out of sight: matching 9mm pistols discreetly tucked into neoprene bands around their bellies. Walter breaks his pledge to be quiet, "If we're looking for gold, shouldn't we have shovels?"

Jamie had started to forget what Walter's voice sounded like, but George, who has a lot riding on this expedition, is eager to share his excitement, "Walter, no offense, but you don't strike me like the kind of kid who could do much with a shovel."

"But how are we going to get the gold out?"

"That's not for today. Today is only to find it."

"Then we come back another day to dig it out?"

"Again, Walter, I'm not sure you'd be much help doing that particular job. We only need you to find the right spot."

"How do I know where the right spot is?"

"When you see something, that's the right spot."

"But it's so big. We could be looking forever."

"When you saw your sister's toy, was your hand right over it?"

Walter faintly remembers that evening, "I don't think so."

"Then today should be no problem."

"But that was a pile of toys. You want me to look underground. That's different."

"The time capsule at the zoo was underground, right?"

"I guess."

"It was under concrete even, so today should be easy, right?"

"Maybe."

George has learned that the more optimistic he is with Walter, the less likely he will get rained on with questions in return. "All we need for you is to find the gold today, and then we're done. That simple."

"And then I can go back to my family?"

"I don't see why not," George responds through clenched teeth.

For the first time since being asked to sign a 6th grader's notebook, Walter flashes a genuine smile. Jamie is astounded by his gullibility. They all stop. In front of them rests the ruins of a structure formerly of the Gold Rush era. Etched onto a slab of weathered granite are words indicating its historical importance. The settlement is now barely more than the scabs of what was; an entryway to a lodging, perhaps, around ten feet tall, with grass crawling halfway up its sides and yellow wildflowers shooting out from its corners.

"Here's a good place," announces George.

"You don't want to try further up?" asks Jamie, motioning to the rolling hills ahead. "This seems too obvious."

"Got to start somewhere." George's energy is too strong to be softened yet. This is his plan. While Jamie is usually a pro at following instructions from Stone, George senses jealousy now that the instructions come from him. Unfazed, he faces Walter, "Alright, kid, do your thing."

Tentatively, Walter lowers himself and sits in the tall grass. The uncut blades provide him with temporary cover from the twins. He takes his right hand and pushes the dense grass down.

"Rip out what you want," George suggests.

Walter attempts to pull the grass from its roots but struggles pitifully. The growth is more unruly than anticipated, so George comes to help. In seconds, there is a bald spot of dirt. Walter tilts his head upward, "Thanks." George grins.

Over the next hour, George and Walter produce various discarded piles of grass and dirt clearings. No gold is found. No vision is had. During these repeated failures, Jamie's body language hardly changes. She's a statue of irritation, an arms-crossed onlooker content to watch George and Walter sweat as her cynicism is further validated. The trio left mid-morning, but now the sun pounds directly above them. Shade is minimal, and they trudge several hundred yards in scattered directions between each attempt. George knows there is no saying about the fifth time being the charm, but as they have now come down the bottom of a hill, physically lower than at any other point so far, he is hopeful (or at least presenting as much).

Sitting once more, Walter takes a deep breath and then gingerly brings his hand upon the overturned soil. He closes his eyes and counts backward from ten in his head. A slight breeze is felt. A hawk crossed their paths twice before but is nowhere to be found now. George is still in anticipation, while Jamie is still as per usual. Walter believes. He wants to see the gold. Making rotations of fifteen degrees to the left and right with his hand, the boy rustles dirt between the spaces of his fingers. He conjures images of shining gold nuggets in his mind but not from underground—from a magazine he once read while waiting for his mom to get off work. Walter takes another deep breath. The hawk calls out somewhere. *Nothing*. Walter opens his eyes, spinning his head towards an anxious George and raising his shoulders apologetically.

"Nothing?" George dreads.

"Nothing," Walter confirms.

George is more than a little disappointed. The sweat coming off him is not 100% the responsibility of the sun anymore. "Give us a sec, Walter," he says in return. The twins walk twenty feet to the edge of shade thrown off by an old oak tree. George stands while Jamie takes a seat on a cool beige rock. A phone call is made.

Over in the grass, Walter cannot hear the twins and quickly stops trying to listen. He chooses instead to lie on his back and stare up at the endless blue of the sky. As there are no clouds to offer distraction, the young boy begins wondering. He wonders how close his mom is to finding him, if Annie notices that he is gone, and if Mitchell is happy to have the room to himself again. Mostly, Walter wonders how long this will take: looking for gold, being away from his family, all of it. In a way, this is what the phone call in progress concerns.

"This was never going to be easy. We wouldn't be the only ones out here looking if it was." George is afraid of losing reception during his call to Stone, so he has his arm uncomfortably folded upward to maintain a connection with some unseen cell tower. Adding to the awkwardness of the conversation, George is also in the uncustomary position of asking his employer to extend a deadline. He suggests that an early start—tomorrow morning, he offers—might allow for a more extensive search and produce more promising results.

"George, it sounds like you're trying to make bad news not sound so bad," Stone counters on the other end, using the burner cellphone retrieved from a secure compartment in his office desk. The graying statesman sits under a stream of cool air as a pair of lobbyists await him in his office's reception area.

"I wouldn't say it's 'bad' news, just no news." George looks at his sister for a reaction, but Jamie is staring miles away. She doesn't have the stomach to face Walter or the care to face her brother. For her, being relegated to the role of driver, babysitter, or bystander is a waste of her talent. What function does this moment serve, she asks herself. *What are we getting from this?* Jamie has seen Walter fail enough to consider this whole endeavor a lost cause. She tells herself that if a tool does not produce, it serves no purpose. *And if it serves no purpose, you get rid of it.*

"Well, it just so happens you have the calendar working in your favor," Stone responds. He is willing to play Monty Hall for the time being. "It's a three-day weekend. I have a lunch—probably will be a long lunch—and that's it until Tuesday. All I want to do between now and then is drink Scotch and sweat it out. If you have your project wrapped up by then, Tuesday morning, you have my blessing. Just—unless things change, don't involve me anymore."

"Tuesday sounds great," George answers in a relieved tone. There are a few tomorrow mornings until Tuesday.

"But George, whichever way it goes, it's finished by then. No loose ends."

"I understand."

Stone doesn't want to keep his lunch guests waiting anymore, so he leaves his underling with a final piece of advice, "And after this is all taken care of, it'd probably be wise to head back to Fresno for a few months."

George offers no immediate reply. Stone takes this silence as confirmation and hangs up. Back in the fruitlessness of the foothills, George swallows uneasily and pockets the phone. A few months sidelined in Fresno is the equivalent of excommunication. As he relays news of the three-day extension to Jamie, he fails to mention any potential homecoming. George knows his sister only operates in a one-way direction, so he applies the same approach he has with Walter: stay positive and don't look too far ahead.

When the twins finish conferring, they head back to Walter, who is unintentionally hidden by the grass. They begin a nervous jog to where they think he should be. "Walter!" George yells out. Slowly, silently, Walter rises, but he is still masked behind a wall of green. Brother and sister look off to the sides, imagining he must have snuck away when they were talking. "Walter!" George is panicking. Jamie is closer to sprinting now. No wedges today. Walter stands. He is clueless as to why his captors look so worried. The yelling stops. The running stops. They reach him, both out of breath.

"What's wrong?"

"Where did you go?" Jamie accuses.

"Go? I didn't go anywhere."

"You're good, Walter," panting, George intervenes as a look of resentment is broadcast across Jamie's face. "We can go now. It's been a long day."

"You mean that's it?"

"Maybe we'll try again in a couple of days."

"And then I can go back with my family?"

"Sure, kid."

The walk back to the car is different for everyone. Walter is relieved, George is worried, and Jamie considers how hard it would be to dig into the hillside. When they reach the lot, Walter informs George, "You know the ones who got the richest off the Gold Rush weren't the miners. It was the people selling the supplies. Most everyone else never found anything." Walter smiles, thinking he has been helpful. George nods, his tension mounting. Jamie calculates: six feet should be manageable.

Chapter 10

Mitchell was a sociable baby. If ever appropriate to describe someone so small as "gregarious," that was Mitchell. He had a smile and a laugh for anyone crossing his path. When Walter crossed his path, coming home after a stint in the NICU, Mitchell carefully inspected him. In return, Walter lay on the ground, looked up at his brother, and cried.

It was hard to help Walter. Instinctively, Mitchell wanted to, but his brother's refusal of anything but his mother's embrace dissuaded him over time. The typical sibling competition for resources only worsened their division; meanwhile, Mitchell had a full calendar of activities, sleepovers, and team sports, while Walter preferred to shelter himself under a book or his mother's protective watch. While Walter looked up to his big brother, he did so secretly. He was envious, even intimidated, by this man-child who walked and talked with charm and confidence while he lay on the ground, looking upward, crying.

Later, Walter would encounter problems at school, but it seemed like business as usual to Mitchell because they seldom confided in each other. Walter received little help elsewhere, as the staff's quick fixes rarely fixed anything, and his parents were either working or decompressing from work. In time, Walter learned to internalize everything. Last October, a month into the school year and a month before their dad would leave to pick up pizza, Walter came to his brother with an issue: the bullying had begun. Terrence and Freddy were starting to mumble and giggle around Walter, a cautious introduction to what was to come. These actions were designed to go undetected by teachers. When Walter spoke to Ms. Meadows about it, nothing happened.

"Terrence and Freddy are making fun of me."

"What are they saying?"

"They aren't saying anything. They're laughing."

"What are they laughing at?"

"Me."

"What are you doing that they're laughing at?"

"I'm not doing anything."

"Then they're probably laughing at something else. Have you talked to them?"

The verbal soon escalated to the physical. If either of Walter's tormentors got up to use the pencil sharpener, they would invariably bump into his desk on the way back. Or, at recess, their running would always veer into his shoulder. Or, in line, they would gently blow on the back of his neck, enough to get a reaction out of him but no one else. Each incident amplified Walter's distress, and with no one at school to believe him and no parent at home ready to hear him, one Saturday morning, Walter built up the nerve to ask his brother for help.

"Mitchell, what do you do if someone messes with you?"

"What do you mean?" Mitchell paused from tying his shoes, unfamiliar with the proposed concept.

"Like, at school, if someone is messing with you, how do you get them to stop?"

"Someone in your class?"

"Yeah."

"Have you talked to Ms. Meadows?" Mitchell figured this revelation of an idea was what Walter needed, so he looped his last lace and made for the door.

"I did. But she didn't help."

"I don't know. Maybe she didn't understand you." And with that, Mitchell was gone.

Walter froze. As he heard his brother walk down the stairs, he imagined Terrence and Freddy laughing. Despite having over half his weekend left, Walter was already dreading Monday. When Sunday arrived, the house lights were off, except for the glow of the TV his dad was watching downstairs. The two boys were lying in their beds when

Walter decided to shut off the thoughts in his head and dare to ask his brother for advice once more.

"Mitchell . . . Mitchell, are you awake?" Mitchell ignored his brother's call. Walter had counted all the times tomorrow that he may have to be near Terrence and Freddy before realizing it was easier to think about all the opportunities he would have to be away from them. "Mitchell, are you up?"

Annoyed by his brother's persistence, Mitchell gave in, "What do you want?"

"Do you know Terrence and Freddy?"

"They're in your grade."

"Yeah, but do you know them?"

"They sometimes play basketball with us."

"Are they mean?"

"Like, when we're playing basketball?"

"Yeah."

"That's not how basketball works. Are they mean to you?"

"Sometimes."

"You should talk to Ms. Meadows then."

Mitchell soon dozed off, while Walter stayed awake until he was the last person up in the house. His anxiety eventually cradled him to sleep and later acted as an alarm clock in the morning. Walter would attempt one more nighttime talk that week, but Mitchell was prepared, ignoring his name being called before Walter reluctantly gave up. With domestic affairs, the two brothers related to each other well enough. However, once they put on their school personas, they spoke a different language or didn't speak at all. That was why Mitchell was shocked to see his brother's costume on the morning of the school's annual Halloween parade.

"Walter, what are you supposed to be?"

"Jason 532."

"Who's that?"

"From *Gravity Slayer.*"

"What's that?"

"Mitchell," Elizabeth, putting the finishing touches on Annie's ladybug costume, interrupted, "that's the series your brother is reading."

Elizabeth's handiwork had produced a more-than-decent half-cyborg, half-rabbit, cloaking talisman included. Walter felt confident in his new body. "Jason 532 is part robot, part giant rabbit. He lives in the Nether Regions of Casseus. You can borrow the books if you want."

In a simple black robe with jagged edges and holding a Ghostface mask with one hand, Mitchell responded with a baffled, "Oh." The disconnect had started earlier that morning.

When Elizabeth dropped her boys off at school, Mitchell ran to his usual group of friends huddled around the basketball court while Walter strolled into Ms. Meadows' classroom to show off his new self for the day. He had told his teacher all about the *Gravity Slayer* series, and, unlike Mitchell, Ms. Meadows listened and even read the first book. After receiving a gracious compliment, Walter left the room quicker than usual, excited to have his costume seen by the rest of the school.

As soon as he reached the blacktop, Walter saw Terrence and Freddy dressed as competing superheroes. As though he had never had one regrettable moment with them, Walter skipped over, beaming. The metallic rabbit ears, the checkered face paint, and the robotic chest plate—it was a good enough costume that the two were too impressed to be their usual selves. Then came the bell, the parade, and morning recess. Then came Terrence and Freddy running. A well-placed bump in the back and Walter, cluelessly standing there, flew three feet forward onto a vacant tetherball court and into its cold metal pole, his nose leading the way. Terrence and Freddy didn't hang around long enough to see the blood gush. Walter's tears mixed with the natural red streaming from his nose and the artificial checkerboard painted on his face. His non-robotic hand pinched his nostrils as he walked dejectedly to the office for an ice pack.

Terrence and Freddy were later called into the office and asked to apologize. They obliged, believably enough for the school administration, and left smirking. Walter decided then to only hover the ice over his nose and knock the top side of his hand into it occasionally, enough to keep the blood going. At lunchtime, Walter was still sitting there, complaining of dizziness, nausea, whatever he needed to say. The school had only been able to leave voicemails for his family about the incident, so they summoned Mitchell to comfort his brother.

Mitchell walked in, mask off but robe still on, and sat in the chair next to Walter.

"What happened?" Now was Walter's turn to employ the silent treatment. "Walter, what happened?"

This is why I needed your help. I knew this was going to happen. Why couldn't you just help?

Silence.

"Have you called Mom or Dad?"

Then it came. Jason 532 reached the entryway to the Stellastar portal. He had grown frustrated by a lack of respect from the Titan squadron leader. "Go away! I don't want you to talk to me. I'm sick of you." Mitchell wanted to say the right thing but did not know where to start. The two Crane boys sat there, neither talking, both looking in opposite directions. They had never been further apart.

***

In the day since Walter's disappearance, his story has been shared online, written about by *The Sacramento Bee*, and covered by local TV stations. The headline "Elementary

Student Missing" triggered parents' worst nightmares. Districts across the region parked security in front of every campus, but attendance dropped 15% after the story broke. This is what the officer assigned to Walter's case is telling Elizabeth when she stops by in the late afternoon of Day 2.

Officer Emma Burton is nearing five years in the Missing Persons Unit. It is not a job she allows herself to discuss when off the clock. Even though many cases are resolved with a happy ending, it's the ones that aren't that stick with her the most. When serving families, Officer Burton has to walk that fine line between being supportive and emotionally attached. As she wraps up at the Crane household, she embraces Elizabeth. Elizabeth needs this hug. Today, she has responded to friends, family, and strangers, many of whom chose to show they care by asking her things she cannot answer. Burton is the first person who has been able to satisfy any of *her* questions.

The house has taken on a tense melancholy in the last 24 hours. After the officer departs, Elizabeth picks up the large manila envelope branded with a red "Missing Persons Unit" stamp on the front. It contains a profile of Walter compiled by the MPU, a resource guide for "Managing this Trying Time," and a printout of the security footage from the school. Elizabeth doesn't know where to put the clasped envelope. She never wants to see it again but knows it cannot leave her sight. Opting to leave it on the living room dresser, Elizabeth walks to the kitchen to pour herself a glass of wine. Annie and Mitchell are upstairs playing LEGOs. Carol is coming over with take-out. It's not even dark outside, but Elizabeth is exhausted.

***

Jimboy's burritos and tacos. Laughter. Carol is saving the day. Annie thrusts her face into her food. Mitchell is doing impersonations. Elizabeth is on her second glass, feeling more relaxed. Then Carol gets up to grab Annie an extra napkin, and Elizabeth sees the empty chair at the table again. With guilt reintroduced, she stops laughing and excuses herself to do the dishes. After dinner, Carol volunteers to put Annie to bed while Mitchell returns to playing in his room. Elizabeth is stuck at the sink. She leaves the hot water to run. Her fingers drip as she puts her hand underneath the heat to see how much she can stand. When the temperature gets too hot, Elizabeth places a small bowl under the stream, it fills up quickly, and the water keeps pouring out.

"Oh my God!" Carol exclaims.

Elizabeth slams off the tap and speeds out of the room. "What happened?!" As she wipes her hand on her shirt, she sees her sister standing there, stunned, holding the manila envelope. Mitchell has slyly crept to the top of the stairs and begun eavesdropping.

"I know this woman," Carol says as she presents the shot of Jamie Bates standing outside of Richfield Elementary.

"What do you mean, you know her?"

"I don't *know* her, but I've seen her before. I recognize her."

"From where?"

"Last night, when I was walking around. I saw her."

"You saw her *last night*?"

"Yeah, that mouth—those glasses. I wouldn't forget. I saw her."

"Carol, I don't—you . . ."

"She was walking by the Capitol by herself."

"The Capitol!"

"Leaving, I think. I don't know. I asked her like I asked everyone last night if she had seen Walter, but she completely ignored me."

"Sis, can you remember *exactly* where you were?"

Carol pauses to think and gestures in the general direction of the Capitol. "On your side, where the sidewalk and the path to the front meet. Near where the little driveway area is."

"I know what you're talking about, Aunt Carol." Mitchell is no longer merely eavesdropping. "That driveway you're talking about, I know where it is."

Elizabeth is too excited to care about her son's sneakiness. She wonders aloud, "Should we call the cops?"

"Do we have enough to tell them?" Carol counters.

"The officer assigned to Walter's case was over here earlier. She seems really nice."

"Okay, but what are you going to tell her? 'My sister saw the person you already have a picture of'? I don't think that helps them."

"We have to do something," Elizabeth knows this much.

Mitchell punctures the room's contemplative silence, "A stakeout!" A confused silence follows. "Dad and I watched these stakeout movies all the time. We go down to the Capitol, to where Aunt Carol saw the woman, and we sit and wait until she comes out again."

Elizabeth is worried that Mitchell may be too immature for this conversation. "Sweetheart, that's not practical. Those people on those shows you watched are law enforcement. What happens if you see the woman again? What are you going to do?"

"Call the cops?"

"So why not call the cops now and tell them?"

Carol is warming up to Mitchell's idea, "Because, Liz, even if they send someone over, they're not going to be here for at least a couple of hours. That woman in the glasses could be there right now. She could be leaving right now. This is about the time I saw her yesterday, remember?"

"So you, the florist, and my eleven-year-old want to stake out a dangerous criminal in your Kia—is that what you're suggesting?"

"Well, when you say it like that . . . yes."

Elizabeth cannot believe she is close to agreeing to this plan.

"It's not a school night, Mom."

"Yeah, Mom, it's not a school night." Carol's sarcasm is easing her sister into acceptance.

"Fine, but here are my rules. One: you leave your phones on as long as you're out. *Both* of you. Two: you don't stay past midnight. And if you see the woman, you call 911 immediately. You don't get out and do anything on your own."

In near unison, Carol and Mitchell answer, "Okay."

"And you have to bring a jacket in case it gets cold." This direction is only intended for Mitchell, but Carol agrees with an exaggerated smile. The stakeout is on. Glass number three is on its way.

***

TIPS FOR CONDUCTING A SUCCESSFUL STAKEOUT:

- Know your purpose;

- Pick a strategic location;
- Pack enough food and water;
- Check that recording equipment is fully charged;
- Bring binoculars;
- Wear comfortable shoes and clothes;
- Set realistic expectations.

The purpose is clear: confirm that the woman captured in the footage from the school is the same woman Carol saw walking around the Capitol yesterday. As far as the right spot, two driveways exit the Capitol on opposite ends of the building. Carol and Mitchell are banking on Jamie leaving from the same exit she was spotted at the day before. If they are unsuccessful tonight, they intend to stakeout the other side tomorrow night. They do not inform Elizabeth of their backup plan.

Because state workers have left for the evening, plenty of parking is available. The intrepid twosome picks a prime spot right before the driveway transitions to the street. They switch the car's lights off and sit in the back, behind partially darkened windows, while, nearby, a changing stoplight is the sole source of outdoor illumination. Bellies are still full of burritos, but Elizabeth insisted they take a thrown-together bag of trail mix: chocolate chips, breakfast cereal, halved cashews, and dehydrated bananas. Water bottles are filled to the brim. Bladders are empty. Their phones are at 100%, and Mitchell wears the binoculars his brother bought in Lake Tahoe three summers ago. As far as realistic expectations, they cannot check that box off.

Mitchell and Carol are convinced they will see those cat-eye sunglasses coming their way as soon as they park. They, however, cannot agree on what they should do next. If they call the cops, sirens might scare the woman away from leading them to Walter, but they are who they are, Carol admits. "How many action movies have you seen where the bad guy is taken down by someone in sweatpants?" They agree to not agree to anything. When—not *if*—they see her, they will snap her picture and then feel out the moment from there.

Carol removes the front headrests to increase visibility, and they sit. And they wait. And within five minutes, they realize sitting and waiting in silence is not a viable option. With her display light covered, Carol presses play on a preloaded playlist. 60s pop songs are selected. Initially, the horn section of The Spiral Staircase reinvigorates the duo, but they soon grow restless again. Carol begins to make a game out of the people walking by, guessing their jobs, relationship statuses, and favorite hobbies. As the night moves on, fewer people pass. They are now listening to 80s hair metal.

At home, Elizabeth rinses the remnants of her fourth glass of wine in the sink and then heads upstairs to check on

Annie. The little girl is sound asleep, limbs sprawled in every conceivable direction. Elizabeth bends over, covers her daughter's feet under a blanket, and gives her a gentle kiss on the forehead. As she stands up, Elizabeth tricks herself into only seeing what's in front of her: her daughter, subdued by sleep, healthy, and within sight.

Elizabeth intentionally has not readied her face for bed because she wants to make sure Carol and Mitchell stick to their promise of a return by midnight. However, that fourth glass and the day's emotions make her eyelids heavy. After moving to her side of the room, Elizabeth leans back against a body pillow and will not wake until morning.

Outside the Capitol, energy levels are fading at a similar rate. It is 10 PM, and Carol is learning you can fall asleep to Tesla's "Modern Day Cowboy." She places the jacket Elizabeth insisted on behind her neck, and soon her eyes flutter shut. Mitchell is okay with his aunt sleeping. He likes the challenge of being the last one awake, the one to crack the case, but he is also struggling. To re-energize himself, he opens the bag of trail mix.

Green and white scooters are the most common attraction of the night. Runners pass by, as do hand-holding couples and a cart-pushing single. Earlier, two cars exited the driveway. The first was a beige sedan with a burly man driving in a suit and a casually-attired blonde on his right. Then came a cleaning van with two uniformed women.

Mitchell asked Carol if these could be their target, maybe in disguise, but she shot down her nephew confidently, "The woman I saw was cold-looking. Like, she wouldn't even blink at a car crash. I could spot her anywhere."

"But you said she was wearing sunglasses?"

"Doesn't matter. I could tell. The older you get, the more people you'll meet. You'll meet a lot of unhappy people in your life, Mitch. And some have even given up pretending about it. She was that type."

Mitchell accepts that one day he may understand. "Aunt Carol, you don't seem like you're ever unhappy."

"I never am when I'm around you guys."

"But mom is. She's sad a lot."

"That's because she's going through a lot. You too. You all are."

"Do you miss Walter?"

"Honey, absolutely, I do. Don't you?"

"I do," Mitchell comes to a half-stop to mull over how much he is willing to reveal. "But I'm not sure if I'm doing it right."

"What do you mean?"

"Mom looks sad. I can tell by looking at her that she misses him. I miss him, but I still see my normal self when I look in the mirror. I tried to make myself look sad earlier but only ended up laughing."

"Don't worry about how you think you're supposed to look. You are Walter's only brother. What you two have, he doesn't have with anyone else."

This had been the last exchange before Carol clocked out for the night. It is 11 now. All the trail mix is gone. Mitchell has been avoiding water, but the saltiness of the cashews leads to his surrender. He is afraid he will have to use the bathroom but is thankful that even a few sips supply him with a jolt. Then gravity and the stillness of the night resume their work, and Mitchell's head begins to fall. He takes a few more drinks before it lowers once more.

Outside, brakes squeak. An SUV is stopped at the end of the driveway by a light. Mitchell pulls up the binoculars hanging around his neck. Through the red glow, he can see the figure of a driver, a woman, maybe. He drops his binoculars to his chest and reaches for his phone. With the camera open, Mitchell pinches the screen to zoom in as the light turns red to green. She is wearing sunglasses.

Click!

Mitchell snaps a series of photos as the car drives out of the frame and down N Street. He inspects his work. Blurry. Dark. Distorted. After consulting the security printout and comparing it to his captures, there is no blur anymore. He sees her, that woman, Jamie Bates. She is in his head. Even if she is not on camera, he knows her now.

Mitchell and Carol never decided what to do if they saw the woman. He nudges his aunt twice but gets no response. Quickly, the adrenaline of the moment wears off, while a second look at his blurry pictures leads to doubt. Now he is jealous of his aunt's sleep.

The center console acts as a pillow as Mitchell rests his head; meanwhile, Jamie is driving to a hotel a few miles away. No one else is in the car with her, but in the back lay two bags full of electronics and food, a folded-up cot, and a children's change of clothes.

Chapter 11

Hours before Jamie clears the room in the garage, she waits alongside her brother and Walter at the front desk of a mid-sized hotel. The boy is decked out in Jamie's sunglasses and George's hat for his brief public appearance. Although the Bates' identities have not been released, they know the boy's face has been distributed to the media by Sac PD.

As Jamie stands in the lobby waiting to check in, her gaze spirals around the hotel entrance. She is sensitive to every potential onlooker, recording device, and window. The second their tenth-floor room door is opened, she snatches back her glasses and slams the rest of the world behind her. Jamie hates to be here. The Westward Hotel is not some two-bit lodging on the outskirts of town; on the contrary, it is sandwiched between a trendy new entertainment complex and the town's most touristy of traps, Old Sacramento. There is potential for exposure on every side. Jamie wants to be back underground and done with Walter already. She, however, is not sure what progress has been made or if any will, and now here they are: in a hotel, in a central part of town, and it is all the boy's fault, again. Or is it George's? She has yet to make up her mind.

George argues that Walter has been unable to perform so far because he is uncomfortable: "It's not every day you get kidnapped. It's not every day you get a bucket to pee in."

"How is that our concern? We didn't promise him anything special like this," Jamie answers back.

"But he's working for us," George responds. "How can we expect him to work under those conditions?"

"There are ways," Jamie says as she grazes the band around her waist.

As the twins talk against the hotel door, Walter watches the blaring TV on the other side of the room, oblivious to the ongoing conversation. George is uncomfortable with his sister's strong-arm tactics, "I don't think we should have to threaten."

"I'm not talking about threatening."

"He's a kid, Jamie."

"Let me just remind you that this was *your* plan."

"Okay, but he's the only one, the only one we've found with this . . . gift."

"What gift? What has he done so far?"

"The box."

"That was a party trick. That's not what the job was. The job was to find gold. Has he found gold?"

"No, but since he'll be more comfortable now, he'll be able to focus better."

"We don't even know how this thing works. We don't know what he needs. And worst of all, he doesn't know either. This hotel room could end up being a really bad idea."

"Or it could be the break we need."

"Or it could lead to nowhere. I think you're too scared to admit that this whole deal was bad from the start."

"Stone didn't think so."

Jamie reveres Stone too much to slander his decision even if he is not present. "Stone also said we have 72 hours left."

"I'm aware. I was on the phone with him."

"So, your plan is room service, cable TV, and then gold?"

"Don't you remember being his age? Wouldn't that stuff have mattered to you?" Jamie pauses. She is not fond of looking backward, but George continues, "I remember us being 10. I remember what motivated us. It wasn't someone threatening me or having to sleep five feet away from my own piss."

"I really can't be here right now. I have to go clean. Enjoy your little trip back to childhood. See if you can get it right this time." George's head drops in exhaustion as Jamie moves to the door. He steps out of her way.

A marathon of *The Twilight Zone* plays on the TV as George takes a seat on the edge of one of the room's two beds. Walter sits in a chair, contorting himself in a way only possible when you are a kid. Turning towards the younger Bates, Walter reassures him, "Don't worry. I have a sister too."

Heartily, George laughs as Walter switches his attention back to the screen. George interrupts, "You want something to eat? They have room service."

Walter replies, "Yes, please," without looking from the TV.

"Anything in particular?"

Walter's response is a silent "not really."

George searches for the room service menu. As he decides on dinner, Jamie departs from the ground floor elevator. Calling her pace "quick" is to call a downpour "wet": it misses the point. Jamie would run from place to place if it were more socially acceptable. She needed to be in the hotel room, and now she needs to call Stone from the car. Everything else is in the way.

Stone immediately recognizes the number on his phone and dispenses with formalities. "Jamie, what's changed?"

"Nothing's changed."

"I talked to your brother a couple hours ago. Did anything change?"

"No, but I thought you needed to know a different side of things."

"Okay." Stone is willing to let Jamie take the conversational lead.

"I know you trust my brother, and you know I am loyal to you but . . . ." When Jamie and Stone typically talk, it is to communicate specific things that have already occurred. *The money was all there. The contract was signed. They won't be pressing charges.* Having to explain her gut is proving more difficult.

"You have your doubts?"

"Yes," Jamie is relieved she did not have to be the one to say it.

"What do you think is going to happen?"

"Well, the kid is on the news already. How did that get out so fast?"

"They're not reporting it as a kidnapping. I was very careful about that. Bullied kid, lost his dad not long ago, stressed about school. The story wrote itself. He's missing. He ran away. Happens all the time. This time it got a little publicity. Don't worry about it. None of the stations are even running a follow-up story today. I gave interviews to them about this bill I'm working on."

Stone's voice is a skeleton key that opens all doors. It's his greatest gift as a politician. Calmed, Jamie tells her boss thanks and starts the SUV. She will spend the rest of the night carefully cleaning every crevice and corner of the room at the Capitol. Nothing will be left behind. Hours later, she will exit with their leftover belongings and a renewed sense of control.

At the hotel, Walter and George are on their third episode of *The Twilight Zone*. A room service dinner of chicken fettuccine and breadsticks has been thoroughly handled. George still feels the heat from the foothills trapped in his skin and wants a shower. He expected his sister to return by now but is also not surprised she overdid it on the cleaning. It has been a personality quirk of hers since before high school.

"Hey, kid, you going to be alright if I take a shower?"

"I'll be fine."

"I can trust you?"

Walter never breaks his concentration from the TV, "Yeah. You can trust me."

When there was a single breadstick left on the room service tray, George offered it to Walter and now is betting on that sacrifice buying him a five-minute shower. He heads to the bathroom with a change of clothes, closes the door most of the way, and runs the water. Moving back to a narrow crack in the door, George looks at the boy still fixated on the screen. If the set were shut off, Walter would be asleep within minutes; for now, he is content to zone out. There is no daring escape in the cards tonight.

When George emerges from the bathroom, he is gratified by his newfound feeling of cleanliness and the trust he put in Walter. *Jamie doesn't know what she's talking about.* A furniture store is advertising its Labor Day sales.

"That room service wasn't bad, was it?" George asks as he pulls up the room's second chair.

"It was good," Walter agrees, readjusting slightly.

"Do you know how to cook?"

"Mostly cereal. I can cook an egg in the microwave."

"How do you do that?"

Walter faces George with his entire focus. He is into this question, "Simple. You spray a round dish and add salt to the bottom. Then you crack the egg, make little holes in it, in the yolk, and cover it with plastic."

"That's it?"

"Microwave it for about 38 seconds."

"38 seconds. Alright then. Where'd you learn that?"

The Twilight Zone returns. It is "Walking Distance" from the show's inaugural season. Walter's focus on George has dwindled back down to sub-50%. "My dad," Walter answers. 25%.

George thinks he has seen this episode before. Gig Young stands outside a merry-go-round, which spins faster than any carousel today would be allowed to go. He sees a boy he recognizes and runs trance-like onto the moving ride. The boy is frightened while the other riders continue methodically moving up and down. They barely appear to be making any forward progress up close but seem to sprint as the camera switches to a wide shot. Terrified by this strange man yelling his name, the boy dismounts and falls to the ground, injuring his leg. Onlookers gasp, and Young reacts as if he also has been hurt. Suddenly, the ride stops. Kids on their basswood steeds stare at the dazed man as though he is a ghost. Young reaches the boy, "I only wanted to tell you that this is a wonderful time of life for you."

George suggests bedtime after the episode ends, and Walter has no argument. He tells the boy to pick where he wants to sleep. Walter chooses the bed nearest the window, which relieves George, as he is unsure how he would justify to Jamie letting Walter sleep next to the door.

"Where are you going to sleep?" Walter wants to know.

"On the ground, probably. I saw some extra blankets in the closet."

"Your sister is going to sleep in the bed?"

"I think so."

"I know when my sister gets cranky that sleeping helps out a lot."

"Let's hope that does the trick," George responds with a smile.

"Is she always like that?"

"Well, she's the older one."

"My brother's older, but he's not mean like that. He definitely acts like he's older, though."

"How much older is he?

"Thirteen months. How much older is your sister?"

"About an hour."

As soon as Walter is in bed, George shuts off the lights. They exchange *good nights*, and George lies on the matching bed, scrolling through his phone, wondering why it takes Jamie four-plus hours to clean a room that's 15 x 15 at most. After confirming that Walter is asleep, George checks all his local news feeds. No updated stories on the kid tonight. He plays a few games, comes close to a high score, and searches "how to microwave an egg." He is grinning when his sister walks in the door. George jumps off the bed.

"He's asleep. How'd the cleaning go?" Before responding, Jamie walks into the bathroom, turns on the light, and waits for George to get the message. He follows her over and whispers, "So?"

Jamie answers as though the bathroom door is soundproof, "It went good. I took care of the video too."

"Is that what took you so long?"

"What took me so long is that I was thorough."

"I didn't mean it that way. Did you eat?"

"I did. Picked something up."

"Nice. We got room service. Watched *The Twilight Zone*, actually."

"So you two had fun?" The word "fun" sounds like a slur coming from Jamie's mouth.

"Why do you say it like that?"

"That's not the job."

"I think it's helping though."

"How?"

"Like I said, if we pick on the kid, it's not going to make things easier. I decided we'll give him a day off tomorrow and then get back to it Sunday."

"Sunday? Isn't that cutting it close? What if Sunday doesn't work out?" Jamie senses her brother's hesitation. "You've started to bond with him."

"You know, sharing a moment of kindness with another human being isn't a terrible thing. Especially for those of us not running on wires."

"You're doing metaphors now? You're never going to be ready for Monday talking like that."

"Let me worry about him, that's all."

"You know that thing under your shirt isn't just for show?"

"He'll come through."

"Even then, that might not change anything."

"Then I'll have a conversation with Stone."

"If you do have that conversation, my advice: no metaphors."

Proud of herself, Jamie excuses George from the bathroom. He moves to the far side of the room, looks at Walter, and then pulls back the curtains to see the Tower Bridge. When Jamie opens the bathroom door, the light shows George's reflection in the glass. She flips the light off and walks to her bed. It is dark again.

Chapter 12

It is one of those days when the clouds cannot make up their mind. The sun comes and goes like a prankish child playing with the lights. George, Jamie, and Walter depart from their hotel for Old Sacramento. Walter is sporting George's hat again, but Jamie has refused to give up her sunglasses this morning.

A piece of public art, an oversized, overturned bronze hand resting in defeat on a raised metal slab, marks the boundary between downtown and the historic district. As they walk, the three pass buildings that resemble a quaint toy set. Eventually, they turn right at the Delta King, the riverboat permanently moored in the Sacramento River. The water is the color of rusted jewelry today, while several snapping turtles crawl across a nearby fallen tree.

Along their walk, a pathway cuts in two directions. One leads to a popular bike trail, and the other dips closer to the water. It would be inaccurate to call this latter option "popular." A large sign reading "NO CAMPING" is posted at the bottom of the slope. Behind it lies 200 feet of quasi-beach. George and Jamie heard "river" and imagined something more spectacular than rugged hills of rock and dirt. They are here to give Walter time outside, some relaxation to go with his night of rest, but the scene they have stumbled upon jeopardizes those plans. "So, kid, here we are," George says, motioning to an even bigger sign proclaiming, "AREA CLOSED." "Your private lap pool has been heated to an ideal 85 degrees." Walter is cracking up. He knows no one swims in the Sacramento River.

The boldfaced signs they passed are displayed to deter the collection of homeless individuals in the area. These notices traditionally have not worked, so speakers that pump out high-pitched noises after dark were installed last year. Though there are only three tents now, the larger communities are found further down, amongst denser plant growth. One man is out of his tent. He lies on a concrete platform with a music case under his head. His shoes are relatively clean. Elsewhere, about fifteen dock rings are positioned throughout the 200 feet of space, memories of a time no current resident would believe. To the right sits the I Street Bridge, brown with age. Opposite this crossing, the art deco-styled Tower Bridge leads cars to and from downtown. Its vertical lift is meant to accommodate large vessels, but today the bridge is only passed under by two men in a personal-sized camo-colored fishing boat. A small wave folds into what barely qualifies for a shore as they putt by.

A second individual then departs from a tent. He is holding a large pillow and yells to the other side of the river, "Don't take those pictures off the shelf!" No one is on the receiving end of his call. Jamie is not worried about him or anyone else on the beach. She figures the homeless want law enforcement poking around just as little as she does.

As the Bateses and the boy move close to the "AREA CLOSED" sign, they are low enough to be cut off from any Old Sacramento lookie-loos. George and Walter take a rocky seat while Jamie leans against a wooden barrier, a trio of water bottles at her feet. The man with the music case leaves. Soon after, the pillow man takes over his perch. Walter asks, "George, how cold do you think the water is?"

"Cold enough that I don't want to find out," George responds.

"Have you been down here before?" George and Walter are surprised to hear Jamie interject anything other than a threat or an insult into the conversation.

"No," Walter answers uneasily. "My aunt has a swimming pool at her apartment. That's where we go."

Jamie has decided that if she does the talking, that means less from her brother. "What's that like?"

"What's *what* like?" Walter wants to know.

"The swimming pool at your aunt's apartment. What's that like?"

"Oh, it's nice. It's not crowded during the day."

"Why is that?"

"I guess most people are at work."

"Does your aunt work?"

"She runs her own business. It's a flower shop."

"What's that like?"

"The flower shop?"

"Yes, the flower shop. What's that like?"

George is dying inside. Walter is trying his best, "It's nice too, I—"

"Walter, you want to skip some rocks?" George comes to the rescue.

"Yes," Walter shoots up as he answers.

"I think we have plenty to choose from." The two leave Jamie behind. She switches her weight between her feet as the clouds come and go and come again.

George and Walter skip rocks, and their record is George's four. Then they underhand toss a few back-and-forth, but accuracy is not Walter's forte. He suggests they have a design-building contest with the materials around them. Minutes into this newest pursuit, Jamie walks over, "George, I think he's turning a little red. Can you go back to the hotel and get sunscreen?"

Looking up from the bottom of his rock tower, George is shocked by such an obvious ploy. When he and Jamie were teenagers, she angrily threw a TV remote at him. The remote hit a wall instead and shattered. As punishment, their father made Jamie stand up and walk to the set whenever the channel needed changing. Jamie's dad hoped she would soon tire of this task and apologize for her temper. No such apology ever came, and George knows there is no use in arguing with her now. Jamie's attention is already back on the water. Turning to Walter, George concedes, "I'll be right back. Five minutes. You probably need the extra time."

"Okay, but don't use it as an excuse when I beat you." The pair exchange a warm laugh that is interrupted once more by Jamie.

"He'll be fine."

Walter keeps his focus on building as George leaves. Shortly after, Jamie kneels next to him, unnoticed. It catches Walter off guard when she speaks. "My brother is not your friend." There is no way for Walter to respond to this, so Jamie continues, "This is not a vacation. You work for us. Do you understand that?" Walter nods instinctively. He is mesmerized by Jamie's tone, which is tense, a projectile speeding towards its target. "I don't think you do. You may be able to joke with my brother, but that's only because he's pretending with you. You don't know who he is. He hurts people. He hurts people for a living. We both do."

The sun breaks from the clouds. Walter, who had been resting his arms at his sides, now has his hands behind him, bracing a row of rocks he set up as a perimeter for the design competition. He stares at Jamie, noticing how big his eyes look in the close-up reflection of her glasses.

"Walter, we are going to kill you."

The boy winces. All sound escapes, and his eyelids close. First, he sees a dark gray flash, and then it happens. He can measure how heavy it feels by sight alone. It is not shining, although it is golden. A sudden jolt causes Walter's neck to strain as a searing pain rushes to his forehead. He makes out two more before his hands push back upon the rocks with such force that he almost lifts himself. Jamie calls his name to no answer.

The man with the pillow has started to notice the commotion. Standing over Walter, Jamie shakes his shoulder with her hand. She yells his name again as he zooms in on the first piece. It is flaking apart. The falling flecks feel like an avalanche from the inside of his vision. Clouds roll in as the pillow man returns to his tent. Jamie runs back to fetch a bottle of water. When she turns around, Walter is lying on the ground, his palms facing up. As she reaches him, Jamie sees that his eyes have opened.

"What happened? Did you see something?"

Walter considers his words carefully, "Thought I did. . . . It was nothing."

Jamie catches her breath. "You need to answer me when I talk to you."

"Sorry, I thought it would be funny."

"It isn't," she says, tossing the bottle at his feet.

When George comes back, this moment goes unmentioned. Later that night, as Jamie is taking a shower, Walter will tell George about the afternoon and those three gold nuggets.

Chapter 13

Elizabeth woke up at 7 AM Saturday to a house that only otherwise had Annie. She panicked and dialed Carol, who apologized profusely (and has not stopped in the two hours since). Carol shook Mitchell awake before they drove home and walked on eggshells through the front door. Mitchell was told to eat breakfast and then go back to sleep upstairs. Carol has not gotten off so easily.

"Obviously, we didn't mean to fall asleep."

"That's not an apology."

"You want me to do that again? I'm sorry. *I'm sorry.*"

"No, I want you to understand how it felt to wake up in a house without two of my kids. But you can't understand that."

"What is that supposed to mean?"

During adolescence, Elizabeth resented how Carol was always over at a friend's house while she was forced to pick up the slack at home. She hated being the eldest, blaming Carol's baby status on the bubble that protected her from any struggle, sweat, or sacrifice. The subject has been broached before, typically in a shared drunken state, but this morning is a starkly sober one.

"It means you don't understand what I'm going through."

"I'm only trying to help."

"Okay. I get that, but—"

"Do you?"

"Yes, you always watch the kids, and I don't know how I would have gotten through this last year without you, but when I woke up and saw two empty beds, I felt—I used to think I couldn't feel worse than last Thanksgiving. Then I didn't think I could feel worse than two days ago. But with Walter gone. Mitchell gone. You gone."

"I'm sorry."

"I also don't appreciate that you took Mitchell's side last night."

"Why didn't you say something?"

"I did. But you got to be fun, no-strings-attached Aunt Carol again, and I played my usual part of the immovable rock."

"So, you're mad that we fell asleep, or are you mad that I came over at all?"

"Stop that. Of course not."

"Well, that's how it sounds. Like I'm not affected by any of this, is that what you're saying?"

"No—"

"Because that no strings stuff is BS. I'm not their mom, but I didn't think I had to be. You know I would do everything I can to keep them safe. I fell asleep. It was a mistake. I'm sorry. But it sounds like maybe this is about something else."

The laundry room they had growing up held a washer that emptied into a sizable in-door sink. One Friday night, Carol started a load before going to the movies with friends. A misplaced sock fell into the drain of the sink, clogging it. Their parents were out at a work event, so when the laundry room started to flood, it fell on Elizabeth to dump the water and mop up the floor. When Carol returned home several hours later, she only asked if her clothes were in the dryer. They never talked about this incident, but it has become Elizabeth's go-to parable when discussing personal responsibility with her children.

"Carol, I am not trying to minimize you or your relationship with the kids. They love you. I love you, but being a parent is different. It just is. I've been on edge every day for almost a year. It used to be that if I was unsure about something, I had someone right next to me to turn to. Now I stay up at night thinking about all the stuff that I'm not going to be able to protect them from. And that was before Walter got taken. So then last night you take Mitchell's side, and the next thing I know, both of you are gone." Elizabeth laughs a sad laugh of desperation as she continues, "I'm on empty, sis, and I don't know how much I have left."

Mitchell is up and has assumed his traditional eavesdropping position. Annie is still asleep, thumb firmly planted in her mouth. Carol, unsure how to respond, pauses before speaking again.

"Liz, stop. Just stop. Do you know how amazing you are? How amazing everything you do for them is?"

"It doesn't feel that way. I couldn't keep Walter safe at school. Not from the woman, not from the kids that pick on him. And that's only the stuff I know about. Only the stuff that's happened so far."

"Walter will come back. I believe that. I do. But beating yourself up now isn't going to hurry things along. You can't skip past the hard stuff. You know that. You've been here before. You always find the strength to go on."

Elizabeth gives a slight nod that Carol tries to believe. The pair embrace. Small tears become lines.

"I love you."

Mitchell tiptoes into the living room and interrupts, "Can I hug too?"

The sisters' embrace opens up. "Of course, sweetheart, come here."

Mid-hug, Mitchell gets curious, "Aunt Carol, did you show Mom the pictures?"

"What pictures?" Mitchell is asked by his mother and aunt together. The hug breaks.

"From last night."

"Mitch, you didn't tell me about any pictures," Carol answers defensively.

"I thought you would have checked my phone. I think I saw the woman. Right before I fell asleep."

Mitchell is back to standing alone while his audience wears a look of guarded optimism. He retrieves his phone and then displays the photos he took last night. They are even harder to make out than he remembers. At best, you can tell there is a vehicle and a body behind the wheel.

"This is it?" Elizabeth returns to being openly pessimistic.

"I know they're not good. But I saw her. The woman Aunt Carol saw. The woman from school. The woman in the glasses. I saw her."

"She was wearing glasses at night?" Elizabeth is proud of her son for wanting to help but is sure he is simply seeing what he thinks will be most helpful.

"Last night, I swear she was."

"Carol, what do you think we should do?"

"Sis, this is all yours."

***

A decision was made not to call the cops. Elizabeth had to deal with a mini-tantrum from Mitchell about "why don't you ever believe me?" At that point, Carol decided to go home. The Cranes have spent the rest of the day not talking to each other. Mitchell is upstairs, sulking and refusing Annie as a playmate. Annie is on her fourth kids' yoga video, while Carol fields a backlog of emails. Officer Burton calls once to check in. Elizabeth does not relay the stakeout information, pretty sure that what her sister and son did crowded the border between illegal and inadvisable. She does not want to lose anyone else's trust at this point.

In the afternoon, the three remaining Cranes eat the quietest PB&Js ever. When dinner rolls around, Elizabeth decides they need a change in scenery and chooses a sushi restaurant in East Sacramento. Moods have calmed by the time the second tuna roll is on the table. On the car ride home, Annie calls out songs from the backseat while Mitchell plays phone DJ in the front. Cake's "Going the Distance" (to Annie, "the race car song") is blasting. Their vehicle passes through the intersection of Alhambra and J Street. A camera flashes from the traffic light above, causing Carol to swear aloud.

"Mom, you said a bad word," Annie notes.

Mitchell turns down the volume.

"Mitchell, did you see the light turn red?"

"I saw it was yellow."

"When I turned, it was yellow, right?"

"That's what I saw."

Another bad word. Elizabeth pulls the car over.

"Mom, what's wrong?" Mitchell asks, unprepared to see his mom distraught once more.

"I messed up again."

"You didn't. You didn't run it. It was yellow."

"They have sensors. It doesn't take your picture unless you run it."

"It was yellow."

"No, Mom screwed up again. Like always."

Walter missing means Mitchell has one less voice to rally with him. "Have you ever had your picture taken before?"

"No, but it's $500, even if it's your first ticket."

"But it was one time. And it was yellow. It wasn't your fault."

Elizabeth looks in her rearview mirror to check for traffic. In the process, her eyes catch Annie, who sits in her car seat smiling, oblivious to the drama around her. *Find the strength*, Elizabeth reminds herself.

The Cranes drive the rest of the way with the music off. Between the lows of the morning and the highs of well-made sushi, they have averaged out for the day. When they arrive back home, Elizabeth decides to call Officer Burton. She wants to get advice on the red light and talk about "the woman in the glasses."

Chapter 14

Walter whispers, “George, I saw the gold.”

“From the hills?”

“No, today.”

“Where?”

“By the water. When it was just me and your sister.”

“Why didn’t you say anything?”

“She scares me.”

“Are you sure you saw it?”

“Yeah, it was like the other times.”

“How much was there?”

The shower turns off in the bathroom, announcing Jamie’s impending return. Walter wants to end this conversation quickly. “Three. Three pieces.”

“That’s it?”

“They were big,” Walters says, lifting his open palm to accentuate his point.

“How far down were they?”

“I don’t know. Can we talk about this later?” Walter motions to the bathroom door. Jamie soon exits while

Walter pretends to be asleep. Five minutes of pretending turn into the real thing.

After ensuring that Walter is done for the night, George approaches his sister in a whisper he adopted from the kid, “Did he tell you?”

“Tell me what?”

“He saw gold. At the water.”

Jamie looks at Walter as if she could tear him apart right there. “That little—”

“Hey, keep it down.”

“I even asked him.”

“I told you he would work out.”

“At least we don’t need him around anymore.”

George begins to consider the implications of this latest development. “Do you think we should tell Stone?”

“Of course, we tell Stone. Why wouldn’t we?”

“No, I was just checking. I’ll call him in the morning.”

“Why not tonight?”

“I’ll call him in the morning. First thing.”

***

Stone enters the Crocker Art Museum with the air of a man for whom all doors open. A woman in her 20s with curls and confidence greets him, “Good morning, Mr. Archer. It’s nice to see you here on a Sunday.”

"It's never too early for a bit of culture," Stone punctuates his remark with a fake but well-meaning laugh. He finds George across the way trying to make sense of a stretching ocean scene. *Is this art? Or just big?* George hears Stone talking at the reception desk, happily turns away from the painting, and acknowledges his boss with a subtle nod.

Departing from the front, Stone walks towards George, who has shifted his attention back to the ocean. The conniving politician passes behind, triggering his henchman to put his head down, count to five, and then follow.

Turning down a corridor, Stone heads away from the renovated building and in the direction of the museum's historic wing. The distanced pair walk through an antique parlor lined with plates and up a winding wood staircase that leads into a gallery room full of opulently framed oversized canvases. Stone stops at *Thunderstorm in the Roman Campagna* by Albert Venus. A shepherd calls his family close as a storm gathers in the distance.

George and Stone do not make eye contact. They face the artwork, though they remain largely oblivious to it. Sunday morning, right after opening, is a quiet time at the museum. A security guard will wander in and out once during their conversation; otherwise, they have the room to themselves.

"So how much?"

"The boy said three pieces."

"That doesn't seem like much."

"He said they were big. Like a fistful. That could mean a kilo or two."

"How much would that be worth?"

"Potentially, $100,000."

Stone nods, "Not bad."

"$100,000 each." George pauses as Stone calculates in his head. "And who knows how much more there is."

Stone walks down the room before settling on *Oedipus and Antigone* by Franz Dietrich. The King of Thebes is depicted in a shameful, wandering state, hiding his crown under a red robe with only his daughter's company to sustain him.

"Have you ever been here before?"

"To the museum? No. Never."

"Well, this building dates back over a century, but the building we were in earlier was finished about ten years ago. I was the one who pushed to get it made." It is hard for politicians to shut off their self-promoting tendencies.

"Impressive."

"You know, anytime you try to change something in the city, people cry foul. They don't want the construction, the traffic, 'what about parking?' It goes on. Then it gets built, and everyone is happy, but no one says, 'thank you.' Now they're talking about expanding the museum to the park across the way, and those same people are coming out again. The construction, the traffic, 'what about the homeless?' Did you know there are 222 public parks in Sacramento? *222*. After it's all done, the homeless will still have more options than they deserve. George, how is it that people that don't pay taxes and don't contribute anything have more rights than the people who make this city run?"

"I don't know," George responds in a tone that is expected of him.

"No one does."

"So what do you do?"

"If it were up to me, you know what I would do. The board of directors, though—they have to be more . . . *diplomatic*. They authorize this study and that study and pledge this money and that. It adds another five years to the process. Slows everything down."

The duo switch to Hermann Kaulbach's *The First Confession*. A gathering of confessors clasp their hands as a young boy in a formal collar looks over his shoulder at a holy card fluttering to the ground. Stone continues, "That's why this news is perfect. We were going to put the squeeze on those coward business owners at the waterfront, but that would probably take at least a year. Now we can give them the one thing that everyone responds to: money. No need to get creative when we have half a million that the Elections Commission can't say boo about."

"Have you thought about how you want me to get the gold out?"

"Isn't that why I pay you?" The religious setting of *The First Confession* has quickly grown unsettling to Stone, so he transitions one painting down to *Sunday Morning in the Mines* by Charles Nahl. The pitting of virtue against corruption in the piece is lost on Stone. He sees only a group of untamed horses and sad-looking men huddled together reading a book.

"I thought about it. Out in the hills, where we were first planning, we had privacy. We don't have that now. Also, the ground isn't dirt. It's solid rock."

"Again, George, this is the job."

In their Fresno days together, George assisted with small-time political foolishness: stolen lawn signs and graffiti; later, he ransacked a rival's campaign headquarters. Stone found in George an initiative that would never penetrate the mainstream but could operate successfully along the margins. He subsequently offered him a more permanent position up north. The pitch was simple, "Do you really want to sell cotton candy for the rest of your life?" George accepted, Jamie followed, and the twins adjusted to Sacramento easily: two drifters in a town with no real identity.

"Okay, so the quickest way to break through would be an explosive of some kind. You still got that guy who did the Watkins ranch in Fair Oaks last year?"

"I can get whoever you need."

"There is one problem though."

"Out with it, son." Stone notices two men bathing on the right side of the painting. He winces, only looking at the frame now, wondering if it is real gold.

"Well, they got all those camps down there."

"Sounds perfect."

"What do you mean?"

"How often do you hear about fires and homeless camps?"

"But this isn't going to be a fire. We're not going to burn the rocks. We're going to have to blow them up. That's going to draw attention."

"People will think it's construction. They'll ignore it."

"And what about the actual people down there?"

"What about them? What about all the needles they leave around town? What about the EPA saying they contaminate the waters? You're asking the wrong questions."

George offers his best bluff, "I only mean that's a lot of witnesses."

"No one will believe what they say anyway."

"What if someone gets hurt?"

"If that's what you're worried about, then don't let someone get hurt."

"Right, but there are people living there. That's all I meant."

"*Living*? Do you hear yourself? They're called 'homeless' for a reason. Kick them out, tell them it's a raid, they're used to it."

Stone's nerves are aggravated by George's sudden excuses and the solemn tone of all these paintings. Anxiousness is not a feeling with which he has much experience. As he walks away, Stone's jaw clenches to stifle stress from reaching the surface. Trailing from behind, George raises his voice enough to give his boss another anxiety spike, "Yeah, but we're not talking about kicking them out. We're talking about explosives near where they sleep."

Stone stops, turns, and makes direct eye contact with George for the first time this morning. Both men stand beside Karl Wilhelm Hübner's *The Village on Fire*. In this action-packed painting, a man holding a child steps down a ladder as smoke envelops buildings in the background. Stone is ready for this meeting to be over. "I didn't know you were such an advocate. What do you think happens to them in the end anyway? Do you know how many vacant buildings there are downtown? Every day, developers sit on their hands, so they can write off those empty parcels as a loss. They make more money that way than they would from a fair-market tenant. Do you know how rare it is for affordable housing to be built down here? Doesn't happen. You know why? This whole town's a set-up. It's the tax law: reward the wealthy, punish the poor. So we're going to interrupt one small section of the riverbank. No one's going to notice the difference, and then they're all going to be happy about it when it's done. It's called progress. At least I'm doing something."

"And what do I do with the boy after tomorrow?"

"Do we need him after tomorrow?" George knows they don't but doesn't want to say so. Stone reads George's non-response. "Look, if you don't think you can handle it, let me know. You got us this far. I'm sure your sister won't mind taking it the rest of the way."

"No, I'll take care of it."

"Glad to hear. I'll have my guy down there at five tomorrow. That should give you a couple of hours ahead of the sun." Before George can confirm, Stone moves back to the staircase, leaving his prodigy behind. The younger Bates is now stuck, unsure how to navigate back to where he started.

***

While George finishes up at the Crocker, Jamie starts in on Walter. The young boy is watching TV, a problem she solves with the press of a button. He looks at her with a questioning face, while her face is all accusations. "You didn't tell me about the gold."

Walter is upset that George didn't keep his secret, but he doesn't have the space to dwell on that, "You said you were going to kill me."

"And you still didn't tell me."

"Why would I? You're not nice like your brother is."

"I thought we went over this already."

"I don't care if he's not my friend, at least he's nice."

"Who drove the car when we took you away? My nice brother did. Whose plan was this in the first place? It was my brother's. Is that who you're talking about?"

"At least George doesn't pick on me."

"Did he tell you where he is right now?"

"No," Walter replies, his curiosity stoked.

"He's meeting with our boss."

"Your boss?"

"Yeah, we don't want you for ourselves. So if you think that I pick on you, imagine the person giving me instructions. That's who you should be afraid of."

After taking a second to consider that there is more to know than he currently does, Walter asks, "What is George doing with him?"

"Now you want information from me? Ha! I asked you about the gold yesterday, and you gave me lies. But now you want something from me!" Walter is silent. Jamie continues, "You're just like George: both so weak. You know, you walked up to me when I was at your school. Why was that?" The intensity builds in her voice. "I think I know. I think you wanted to come with me. I don't think you want to go home. You don't like your family and want to be done with them, is that right?"

"Stop it! Stop always talking to me!" Walter yells ferociously in Jamie's direction. In opposition to the laws of acoustics, the modest hotel room seems to echo.

Jamie relents, nodding, half mockingly, half in approval. "George will be back soon. I'm sure there will be plenty to talk about then." She tosses the remote back to Walter and proceeds to the bathroom. With the door closed behind her, Jamie removes her sunglasses, acclimates to the harsh fluorescent lighting, and grabs a pair of tweezers. She leans over to the mirror, plucks two out-of-place hairs, and straightens up to appraise her reflection.

Back in the room, the TV is still switched off, and Walter has not moved. The boy's eyes are fixated on the ceiling. There are a million tiny bumps up there, but he isn't counting a single one.

Chapter 15

At 12, Jamie got her first pair of sunglasses from her stepmom. They were whatever is between a peace offering and a bribe: "I don't have to be your new mom, but please stop slamming the door in my face." Promptly, Jamie shoved the glasses in the bottom of a dresser drawer, and there a pair of polarized Maui Jims sat for months until they were brought up at dinner one night, "Jamie, how come you don't ever wear those sunglasses I gave you? You need to protect your eyes." A door was slammed seconds later. Jamie's stepmom wasn't so mad that her money and employee discount were going to waste, but it had been six months in the same household and six months of being treated like an intruder. Later that night, the sunglasses found their way outside to the top of a bin reserved for recycling. Soon after, they were retrieved and discreetly put back into the dresser drawer, although they were not the subject of further dinner-time discussions.

In contrast, George got along with his new step-parent. His "gift," a refurbished Nintendo DS, was happily accepted. George also found himself untouched by the middle school ridicule his sister faced. While Jamie dealt with comments about being a "freak" or taunts of "your mom's a schizo," George's thick skin and agreeable manner allowed him to make friends with anyone.

One morning, after predicting the day's remarks in her head, Jamie reached for her dresser drawer and the glasses she knew her stepmom had snuck inside. Opening the case in careful anticipation, Jamie put on the Artic blue frames and walked cautiously to the bathroom. Upon inspection, she looked—well, she looked like she was wearing a $300 pair of sunglasses, and that was a good enough change for her.

When Jamie arrived at school, she expected the entire student body to be chanting "poser" or worse; to her surprise, they said nothing. They did not celebrate or attack but left her alone, which was good enough again. On the other hand, her stepmom noticed immediately. After returning from school that day, Jamie opted to leave her Maui Jim's on, so when her stepmom saw her sitting on the couch in sunglasses, she did a double-take, "Jamie, you look nice." Jamie responded with a polite smile. That was good enough for them.

Jamie sets her glasses down tonight after switching off the bedside table lamp. George crawls over in near-darkness as streetlights sneak in through cheap curtains. He rebuffed earlier invitations for conversation, so as he suddenly announces to his sister, “we need to talk,” Jamie is annoyed.

“Can we do this in the morning? You had me all day with the kid.”

“I know, but I was waiting for him to fall asleep.”

Jamie reluctantly sits up and blindly reaches for her glasses until her brother’s left hand stops her. With his right, he grabs the glasses for himself. “What are you doing?” she wants to know.

“This will only take a minute. Just come outside.”

“Outside?”

George tosses his sister’s eyewear onto a pillow and leads Jamie out of the room. The bulbs that line the empty hallway are dim. Jamie braces herself against the door, her head slightly downward.

“What are we doing all this for?” George begins.

“All of what?”

“This, the kid, the job with the paralegal last month. Why do we do it?”

“Because Stone pays us to.”

“Okay, but why do we work for him?”

“What are you asking?”

“Just answer: why do we do this?”

“For the money of course.”

“But we could get other jobs, right? We don’t live hella lavishly or anything.”

"What other jobs?"

"I don't know. I just know I don't want to go on like this anymore."

"Are you religious now?"

"I'm just saying, why does this have to be all we do? Like, what if I never met Stone? What would we be doing then?"

"If you had never met Stone? Stone is the best thing to happen to us."

"I don't believe that."

"What were you doing in high school? You were doing stuff then like what we're doing now. Only difference is now you get real money for it."

"What about you?"

"What about me? Don't worry about me. I'm not the one who's scared."

"But why do you always have to go along with what Stone says?"

"Because he's the boss. That's the job."

"No, that's not it."

"Then tell me."

"You can't live without someone telling you what to do."

"You don't know what you're talking about."

"Used to be Dad, now it's Stone." Jamie dismissively laughs as George continues, "You're incapable of making a choice for yourself."

"I choose to do all the hard work you can't do. That's a choice: making you think you're necessary when really I could do it all by myself."

George is well aware his sister's stubbornness isn't going to change course through mere conversation. "Jamie, I love you, but I'm done working for Stone."

"Why now?"

"He's asking me to do things I'm not going to do."

"Is this the plan you refused to tell me about earlier?"

"I'm done is all you need to know."

"Did you tell him?"

"No, but I'm not showing up tomorrow."

"So, I get to clean-up everything? As usual."

"No, I want you to quit too."

"Quit what? Did you ever think to ask if I wanted to?"

"I know you don't want to. But that's what the money's for."

"What money?"

"I took out as much as I could at the ATM today. It's not a lot but consider it a down payment. It's in an envelope in the desk. I also put a check in there for the rest of what I have. Everything I've ever saved. That should double what you have now and make it so that you can go off to do whatever." Jamie shakes her head in disbelief and begins opening the door back to the room. George pulls it shut before his sister can enter. "Jamie! If you do this, you get what I want, and I—"

"Don't pretend to be an expert on me."

"You can take the car too."

"How long have you been planning this?"

"Not long."

"It shows."

"Jamie—"

"And what are *you* going to do?"

"I'll manage."

"Manage?"

"I'll keep myself safe and you too."

"But what about the kid? He knows what we look like. Our names."

"Leave him to me."

"This is ridiculous."

"No, it's simple. Take the keys and the envelope and never look back."

"You haven't thought this through."

"I thought about what Stone's asking me to do, and I can't do it."

"So just tell me. I'll do it."

Faint light peers in through the cracks of the closed door. George opens it enough to make sure the boy is still asleep. Walter's eyes are shut, and his breathing appears calm. "The kid told me you threatened him yesterday. Only I know you would never do it."

"You don't know me as much as you think you do."

In an instant, George begins to believe that maybe he doesn't. "What do you mean?"

"You and I don't do the same work."

"Because you clean?"

"I'm not talking about that."

"Then what?"

"No."

"Then what, Jamie?"

"You remember last winter, when Stone called me down to LA for the week?"

"Vaguely," George is on fragile ground now. "The donor's mistress or something? You got her to sign papers?"

"Not exactly."

"I don't understand."

"Stone and I both know there are certain things you won't do."

"What are you saying?"

"I'm saying I'm Stone's safety net for moments like this."

"No, that's not who you are."

"Correction: that's not who you want me to be."

"So what did you do down there?"

"Doesn't matter now."

"Jamie, what did you do?"

"When people stand in your way, all it takes is a little push."

"I don't—you've never said anything about that. You—"

"I killed her, George. She's dead. It was easier that way." George has no words, so Jamie continues, "Stone and I both agreed you wouldn't understand, so we didn't tell you."

After a brief pause, George grows increasingly desperate, "Okay, but we're talking about a kid now."

"What's the difference?"

"He's a kid."

"I heard what you said. You heard what I said. Stop being sentimental."

"Take everything, Jamie. Quit talking like that and take everything."

"I'm going to bed."

"Jamie—"

"I'm going to bed."

George is done. The ground has collapsed around him. Eventually, he recalibrates, sets his alarm for 3 AM, and lies down for what's left of the night. As he rests his head,

George feels the glasses he tossed down earlier against the side of his face. He grabs them, gets up, and walks to his sister's side table. After placing the frames down, one end at a time, George lets go completely, "Goodnight."

***

On the night before everything will change, Sacramento lies in waiting:

. . . cars are stuck at red lights on empty roads;
. . . apartment sprinklers flood the city's sidewalks;
. . . fresh donuts are pulled from the oven at Marie's;
. . . vendors at the Labor Day festival prep supplies;
. . . a homeless man with burn marks rakes up leaves;
. . . Security at East Lawn Mortuary does its rounds;
. . . a mechanic wires a switch to an explosive device;
. . . Officer Burton laughs contentedly at reality TV;
. . . Annie snuggles against her favorite pillow;
. . . Mitchell looks at his bedroom clock in defiance;
. . . Carol double-checks an order of zinnias;
. . . Terrence and Freddy play online video games;
. . . Elizabeth logs into a virtual support group;
. . . Stone exits the sauna at Capitol Heritage Club;
. . . George snores as a lone ant crawls up his ankle;
. . . Walter dreams of a snake slithering free;
. . . and Jamie walks to the car, a hastily-made bag in one hand and a stuffed envelope in the other.

Chapter 16

The vibrations startle George awake. Haphazardly, he reaches for where he last recalls leaving his phone. After silencing its alarm, the early morning comes into focus. He pushes himself up and scans Jamie's bed. *Empty. No glasses on the table.* He walks over to the desk. *A bible and pamphlets for local businesses. No envelope.* George hopes this means Jamie has left to disappear and not to talk to Stone. There is no surprise or hurt that she would have gone so suddenly. You don't get to pick your family. You can only try to understand them.

George glances over at Walter. He has to wake him up soon but wants to avoid it for the moment; instead, he reaches for a leftover grocery bag, filling it with a bottle of water and the last pack of trail mix. Because further delays could complicate what is destined to be a complicated day, the lights are switched on, and Walter's left shoulder is gently nudged. "Walter . . . Walter, time to wake up," George whispers. *No response.* Walter, sleeping on his side, is now prodded more forcibly, "Kid, we got to wake up. We got to go." Hazily, Walter opens his eyes. Sitting on the bed, George has his head positioned directly over Walter and in front of the ceiling's harsh light.

"What time is it?"

"It's early but . . . " before George can fully answer, Walter drapes his head onto George's leg and closes his eyes once more. George allows himself a brief chuckle and then stands, letting Walter's head fall to the mattress. "Kid, you got to get up." He pulls back the top blanket and walks to the bathroom. After reemerging with a glass of water, he hands it to Walter. It takes two gulps for the young boy to be present.

"Why is it so early?"

"I'll explain in a minute. First, you got to get dressed. Your clothes are in the bathroom. Do all that, and then we'll talk."

"Okay."

When Walter returns from the bathroom, he is wearing his first-day-of-school outfit again. There are more wrinkles, and his hair is messy, but it is a weird flashback to what life was like mere days ago.

"You get to go home today."

Walter is now fully awake, "I do?"

"Yup, you did your job. You found the gold. That's all we needed, remember?"

"What about your sister?"

"Don't worry about my sister. She's not really like that."

"When do I get to leave?"

"The good news is you get to go now. The bad news is you have to walk home by yourself. Do you think you can find it from here?"

"Where are we?"

Innocent question. George laughs, "You live by the Capitol, right?"

"I think, like two or three blocks away."

"If you can get to the Capitol, can you get home?"

"Yeah."

"Okay. Tell me."

Walter begins motioning with his hand as he considers his route back. "At the Capitol, you walk up the side, the right side. Go like halfway. Past the light rail stop. Then cross by where they're doing construction. Past the parking lot, past the laundry place, the smoothie place, the restaurant, and cross the street. Walk a little bit more and then turn left. I live in the five, six, seven, eight—eighth house."

"Alright, so let's figure out how to make it to the Capitol." The two spend the next few minutes looking at an online street map to plot the simple steps needed to get Walter home. Once he leaves the hotel, it is a straight shot through the nearby mall and down K Street. "When you see the Capitol on your right, turn and start walking towards it." Walter nods confidently and begins putting on his shoes.

As his last lace is looped, Walter's curiosity gets the better of him, "Who's Stone?"

"Who?" George hopes playing dumb will work.

"Stone. You and your sister were talking about him last night."

"You heard that?"

"She's not very good at whispering."

"It's probably best that you forget that name."

"Is he your boss? Your sister said you had a boss."

"Did she? It's something like that."

"Is he going to be mad at you for letting me go?"

"He's probably going to be mad for a lot of different reasons, none of which are your fault."

"I . . ."

Nodding, George reassures the boy, "It'll be fine. Sometimes you just got to deal with the hard stuff." After drifting away momentarily, George returns to the task at hand. "You're a good kid, Walter. Now let's get you back to your family."

"Okay."

George picks up the packed bag and hands it to Walter before opening the door. "Thanks," Walter says as he accepts. It is all hallways from here.

"Alright, kid."

Walter takes two steps and turns around. George nods, causing Walter to smile.

"Be safe."

"You too."

George steps back while Walter stands a second longer before continuing down the hall. He hears the door closing behind him but does not turn around.

The walk down K Street is intimidating. There is a chill in the air, and the moon is still out. Walter has done this walk enough when visiting his mom at work or going to the movies, but he is alone and in the dark this time. As he passes storefront after storefront, some vacant, others recently developed, his biggest takeaway is the large number of people who call these streets home. Walter counts no less than a dozen individuals and one couple huddled against the doors and plywood boards throughout the block. They have found refuge in front of churches, phone repair shops, and art galleries. Yoga mats, tarps, and sleeping bags provide their cushion, while their personal belongings are kept in carts, backpacks, and garbage bags. One man has cornered off his cubby hole of space with bungee cords. Here Walter places the bag of food and water George prepared, freeing him to plant his hands in his pants pockets. There is the early morning temperature to contend with, but Walter also wants to make himself as unnoticeable as possible. Hunched over, the boy walks with his head down and eyes darting left and right. The stench of urine hits him hardest when the breeze kicks up.

As Walter reaches 10th & K, the Capitol comes into view like distant land sighted by an ocean explorer. He crosses the street hurriedly and begins his trek through Capitol Park, sensing how close he is. A bearded man in a Sacramento Kings sweatshirt has fallen asleep not far from a family gathering of raccoons. Walter walks on. He sees a woman wearing a lacquered bouffant hairstyle dressed for her first day of work in 1964. She is awake, rocking on a park bench back and forth, back and forth, while a faded rolling suitcase sits at her side. Walter spots the street ahead and knows he can run the rest of the way.

After checking the one-way traffic along N, Walter gives himself the "all clear." He sprints. It's a PE sprint, a last-day-of-school sprint, a mom-and-dad-are-home sprint. His hands are out of his pockets—the laundromat, the smoothie place, and the restaurant pass in a blur. No cars. Walter cuts diagonally across the street and leaps onto the curb. He pictures the door open. He wants to see it open. He will ring the bell. The door will open.

Walter is out of breath as he manages the side street that leads to his house. A motion detector is set off at 1106 Coach Way. 1114 is the goal. He reaches the outside gate. The house is still. He sees the car, the rocks that line the yard, and the chalk drawings he drew on the walkway with his brother and sister only last week. They are faded, but he can make out the superhero sketches and fairytale castles. He rings the bell and hears the chiming from outside.

Inside, Mitchell hears nothing. Annie hears nothing. Elizabeth loses a layer of sleep. The bell rings again as she opens her eyes and checks her phone. No messages. *What was that?* Then the third ring comes. Elizabeth mutters about how early it is while she throws on a robe to investigate. She trudges downstairs as Walter pushes the doorbell for the fourth time.

"Alright, I'm coming."

Elizabeth reaches the door, stands on her toes, and looks through the peephole. Though its concave lens distorts the outside and the darkness makes it difficult to see, Elizabeth sees. There, twenty feet away, spotlighted from the bulb on top of the outside gated door is—

"WALTER!"

The deadbolt is flipped. Then it happens. The door opens. It opens, and Elizabeth runs to Walter. She unlocks the outside gate and throws her arms around her missing boy. There will be time for questions and stories later. There will be time for everything else. Right now, this is all there is.

Chapter 17

Reunited and hungry, the Crane children devour their peanut butter and jellies. When presented with the option of eating whatever he wanted, Elizabeth thought Walter would decide upon something extravagant; instead, he chose to stay home with sandwiches. As crusts are finished, the doorbell rings. A recently returned Aunt Carol checks through the window and buzzes in Officer Burton.

"Carol, can you take Annie and Mitchell upstairs?" Elizabeth asks from the kitchen.

Before Carol can answer, Annie protests, "Can Walter come too?" She grabs hold of Walter's legs.

"Your brother needs to talk to someone, and then he can," Elizabeth informs her eager daughter.

"Can I talk to someone?" Annie quips back.

Carol jumps in, "Annie, how about you play an awesome game with Mitchell and me?"

"What game is it?"

"It's called The Awesome Game."

"Oh, sure, sure, that's my favorite. Bye, Walter."

As Mitchell follows his sister upstairs, he turns to his little brother, "Good luck, dude."

Walter smiles proudly.

The room's energy changes as Carol herds the troops upstairs. Burton's pulled-back hair and notepad denote a seriousness that is an awkward transition from leg hugs and PB&Js.

"Hi, Walter, my name is Emma," Burton introduces herself, extending a hand. "It seems like your family missed you a lot."

"Yeah," Walter shakes back with a satisfied look.

"Can I get you anything?" Elizabeth volunteers.

"Thanks, but I'm alright for now. Walter, do you mind if I sit?"

Walter points to the nearest seat, "That's where Mitchell sits."

"And what about you?"

"Here."

Officer Burton sits, and Walter follows. Elizabeth assumes her usual position at the head of the table.

"So, Walter, let me tell you a little about myself. My job is to help families like yours. If someone goes missing, it's my job to find them and bring them back home. When your mom called this morning, I was excited. It seems like you did my job for me." Walter nervously looks at his mom. "I wanted to stop by and ask a few questions. Your mom thought that would be okay. Do you think it would?"

Walter defers to his mom, who reminds him, "She's asking you, sweetie."

"It's okay."

"Great. Before I start, I want you to know that if you need a break, that's perfectly fine. If you want to skip a question and come back to it, that's also fine. But I do have to tell you that these questions are not only for your mom and me. I work for the police, and it's our job to keep everyone safe. It seems there are some bad people out there that we need to find so that we can keep doing that. Do you understand?"

Walter meekly nods while Elizabeth adds, "And Walter, if you need me to leave so that you can speak to Officer Burton by yourself, I will understand."

"Mom, I want you to stay." There is nothing meek about Walter's response this time.

"Definitely. I want your mom to stay too. I think we can all agree that you've spent too much time away from her recently." The nod returns. "Walter, I'm going to start by asking what you remember about the woman who took you from school last Thursday." Walter looks like he has been paused. No reaction registers at all. "How about I show you a picture, and then you can tell me what you remember?" Officer Burton pulls out the photograph from the school camera and sets it in front of Walter, pushing a few stray sandwich crumbs to the side.

Walter studies the picture. It is a poor shot of Jamie, but he can still imagine her kneeling next to him. He offers a calculated answer, "Actually, I don't remember that well anymore. I hit my head at the end of school last year."

"You're saying that you have trouble remembering sometimes?"

"Sometimes."

A skeptical Elizabeth squints her eyes and shakes her head "no" for Burton to see.

"Well, take a second and look at the picture. For instance, her glasses, do you remember what she looked like without her glasses?"

"No. I don't."

"Okay. Eye color can be tricky. What about how she acted? Was she nice? Was she mean? How did she treat you?"

"I don't remember."

"Walter, are you thinking before you answer?" a frustrated Elizabeth interrupts.

"Mom, I don't remember." Walter is fidgeting with the fabric lining in his pants pockets.

"What about, do you remember hearing her name or going anywhere with her?" Burton's follow-up causes Walter's head to collapse. Seeing where this is going, she detours, "Walter, how about you check on how your sister and brother are doing? Your mom will get you when we're ready to start again."

In second grade, Walter was called to the teacher's desk. He had forgotten to complete an assignment and sat there paralyzed, convinced that a prison searchlight would expose him to the world. That slow, guilty walk he took to the front of the room has returned. Once Walter is confirmed upstairs, Elizabeth begins apologizing. "I'm so sorry. I don't know what's going on. I know he knows more than what he's saying."

"Probably nerves," Burton defends, scooping Jamie's picture back from the table. "Did he mention anything to you before I came?"

"No, but I didn't really ask him. I was going to leave that to you."

"Absolutely. Well, in a minute, I'll try a different approach. If that isn't working, we'll hit the eject button and try again tomorrow."

"Okay. Again, I'm so sorry."

"Stop apologizing. You haven't done anything wrong." Burton speaks so confidently that Elizabeth almost allows herself to believe these words. "How are you doing?"

"This morning has been crazy. But in a good way, obviously."

"I bet. And it's nice that you're so close to your sister."

"It is. She's been amazing. I can't imagine going through this whole thing alone. I mean, I have Annie and Mitchell, but—"

"I know what you mean. It's good to have people."

"It really is."

"Alright, let's try calling Walter back down now." While Elizabeth retrieves Walter from upstairs, Officer Burton preps herself for a new angle. The boy returns to his seat as his mom's hand encouragingly grazes against his. She gave him a mini-pep talk before coming down and is hopeful it will pay off.

"Sorry, for earlier," Walter begins. "I was a little nervous."

"I see apologizing is a family thing, " Burton remarks with a smile towards Elizabeth, who uses all her power not to apologize back. "Walter, you've done nothing wrong. Not today. Not last Thursday. I know you've been through a lot. You mentioned earlier that you hit your head not too long ago?"

"It wasn't that bad."

"Oh, your mom told me that you had to spend some time in the hospital."

"Yeah. But I'm better now."

"If you don't mind me asking, how did you hit your head?"

"On a field trip."

"A field trip? Sounds like fun. Where'd you go?"

"The railroad museum."

"You slipped and hit your head at the museum?"

"Not really."

"Okay. How did it happen then?" Elizabeth told Officer Burton this story not long after their first meeting.

"Well," Walter turns to study his mom's face before continuing, "A couple of boys pushed me."

"Pushed you? That must have hurt."

"It did. I was in the hospital for a while. I got knocked out."

"That's horrible. Now, Walter, if you don't mind me asking, why did those boys push you?"

"Bullies, I guess."

"Sounds like it. Do you know what happened to them?"

"What do you mean?"

"Did they get in trouble or anything?"

"They didn't really."

"And how did that make you feel, that those two, those two bullies, could do something so bad and not get into any trouble for it?"

"I—I hated it. They always pick on me. And the school doesn't do anything. It's not right."

"You know what, Walter, I agree."

"Thanks," the boy responds sincerely.

"And part of why I became a police officer was to help people who had been treated unfairly, to make sure that things like what happened to you don't get to happen again." Walter supports this mission statement. "So, earlier, I was asking you about the woman who took you from school, and you said you didn't remember her. But maybe now, can you think about it again?" The air is let out of the room once more. Burton notices, "Take your time."

A carousel of memories is spinning through Walter's head: Jamie's hand on his shoulder, forcing him away from school. The loud music in the car as George drove away. The bucket in the corner. The soggy fries. Lying in the tall grass. The hotel room. Skipping rocks. "We are going to kill you." Walter has been up since 3 AM and still feels sewn to George and Jamie. "I remember the woman a little bit. She wasn't nice, and she wore glasses all the time, even inside. But I don't remember anything else. And she wasn't around very much. She took me someplace and then left. I never saw her again."

"How did she take you away from the school?"

"In a car."

"Who drove the car?"

"She did."

"She took you from the school *and* drove you away?" Walter confirms. "And this place where she took you, what do you remember about it?"

"Not much. It was dark. I was blindfolded. I had headphones over my ears. My hands were tied." As Walter talks, Burton looks down at his wrists. *No markings*.

"When you got to where she was taking you, how big was the room you were in?"

"Pretty small."

"And she left you there by yourself?"

"Yeah, there was a bed. Oh, and a bucket to use the bathroom in."

"Sounds awful. You were gone for three whole days, so what kind of food did you eat?"

"Mostly, sandwiches."

"Oh yeah? What kind?"

"I don't really remember. They weren't very good. I didn't eat much."

"And this woman brought you the food or someone else did?"

"She did."

"I thought you said you didn't see her much."

"Well, I didn't. She slid the food in through a hole in the door."

"I see, and when you weren't eating, what were you allowed to do?"

"Nothing."

"Nothing?"

"I guess I could draw."

"Oh, there were things for you to draw with?"

"Yeah. Chalk."

"And paper?"

"No, I could draw on the walls."

"And what kind of pictures did you draw on the walls?"

"Mostly, comic book stuff."

"But you couldn't have drawn too much, right? Because the room was so small."

"Well, they gave me an eraser, so I could keep drawing."

"'They'?"

"What?"

"You said 'they' gave you an eraser? Was someone else with the woman?"

"I don't remember." After that day in second grade, Walter never let an assignment linger again. He wishes this interview could go differently but doesn't see another option.

Elizabeth cuts in, "Walter, we said we weren't going to do 'I don't know' answers anymore, right?"

"Right. I'm sorry. There *was* someone else, I forgot."

"Great job remembering, Walter," Burton oversells. "Do you remember anything about this other person? How about, was it a man or a woman?"

"A man."

"Excellent. And what do you remember about him?"

Sometimes you just got to deal with the hard stuff.

"He was big. Older."

"Do you remember what color his skin was or what kind of hair he had?"

"It was dark in the room. But he was meaner than the woman. He was the boss. He gave her directions. He was in charge of the whole thing. It was his idea."

"What was?"

"Taking me."

"Did he say why they were taking you?"

"To get money."

Burton slowly closes her eyes, feeling like all forward progress has been lost. As no ransom was ever demanded, nothing about Walter's answer or how he answers rings true to her. She's ready to go back, write her report, and hope paths open up elsewhere. "Okay, well, I want to say thank you for sharing, Walter. I think you've been really brave and given me about all I need. Before you go upstairs to play though, can you tell me, if you remember, what the man's name might have been?"

"His name?"

"Yes, maybe something the woman called him? Something you might have overheard?"

Walter pauses, his eyes stretching in size, "Stone."

"Stone?"

"Yeah. It was Stone."

"Thanks, Walter, I think I have enough now. Unless your mom needs you, you're all done down here."

"Go play, sweetie." Walter races up the stairs. A burst of excitement is heard when he opens the door. Burton and Elizabeth stare at each other, both more tired than thirty minutes ago.

"I know I have a habit of apologizing, but I don't know what else to say. I don't understand why he wouldn't answer your questions."

"Maybe he did in his sort of way. We'll just be on the lookout for a mean woman and an even meaner, older man." The two share a laugh that burns like bile in the throat when it dies down.

"You know, the night before Walter was taken, the kids were doing chalk outside. And he always draws characters from his comic books."

"I noticed that on the way in."

"And I don't know if you saw this too, but grass doesn't grow in our yard, so we have a lot of rocks."

"He did say 'Stone,' though."

"Even worse of a lie if you ask me."

"It's weird actually. Have you had the TV on today?"

"No, we've been too busy. Did something happen?"

Officer Burton pulls out her phone. She does a quick search, clicks, and hands her device across the table.

SENATE LEADER ARCHER MURDERED

President of the State Senate, Stone Archer, was killed by a gunman who turned a peaceful Labor Day morning into a deadly crime scene.

Elizabeth looks up from reading, "This happened today?"

"This morning. It's all over the news right now. Archer was a big deal."

"I know. I saw him this weekend talking about his plan for the homeless."

"Exactly, and who knows what happens now?"

"It's a shame, but you don't think Walter—we haven't had the TV on all day. "

"No, probably a weird coincidence. Rock, Stone, like you said. Anyway, I'm going to head out. If he shares anything with you later, you have my number and email."

"I do."

"But don't feel like you have to pressure him. I'm sure we'll get some descriptions or names out of him eventually."

Chapter 18

Last week, Walter lay in bed, nervous about the first day of school. As he faces a return to Richfield, those little pinging balls that bounce around inside have begun to settle down; whereas Walter previously took for granted the strength that came from home, now he is drawing from it. He walks around his house trading random *hello's* with Annie and Mitchell and hugging his mom without warning. The reassurance that comes from these exchanges gives him newfound powers.

Walter is aware of the media attention his story has received. A counter full of flowers and cards is tangible evidence of his growing public reputation, but he is finished being treated like the odd kid out. The post-zoo interview hubbub that met him last week was enough. He is through being Walter the kid on TV or Walter the kid who went missing, and he's absolutely done being Walter the pushover. He considers allowing his "hand sight" to be his new calling card but does not want the accompanying baggage. These thoughts pulse through his brain when he bows out of a mini-basketball contest with Mitchell and Annie to join his mom downstairs.

"Mom, can we talk?"

Elizabeth looks up from the bloated inbox looming on her laptop. "Of course, honey, what's up?"

Walter sits, "Do you have anything that makes you special?"

Elizabeth chuckles as she closes her laptop. *Innocent question*. "Well, sweetheart, I would like to believe that being your mom makes me special."

"I don't mean stuff like that. Like, talents?"

"Oh. I can type pretty fast. And I predicted the dates of when all three of you were going to be born."

"Anything like with my hands?"

"What do you mean?"

"Mom, my hands, how I can see through things."

It takes Elizabeth a second to make sense of this comment. If she is honest, the zoo feels like forever and a half ago. "That's right. You're still doing that?"

"I can't really control it, but when I was gone, I did it a couple of times."

"You did? Walter, how come you didn't mention that to the officer?"

"I did. I said they wanted me because of money. They were using my hands to find money."

"You found money?"

"Not really. But I don't want to talk about it."

"Okay, we can talk about it later then." Elizabeth does not believe that anyone can do what Walter describes, but more than that, she does not want to embrace the possibility that he will stand out in yet another way. Like most parents, Elizabeth wants her son to grow up and be unique, but she also knows this world tends to punish those who parade too proudly what makes them unique. Walter does not need to be a part of the crowd—the periphery would be fine—but what he is suggesting, Elizabeth fears, is the stuff of desert islands.

"Did Dad have any talents like me?"

"Actually, in a weird way, yes. Your dad was a tetrachromat."

"A *tetra-what*?"

"A *tetrachromat*. He had an extra cone cell in his eye, so he could see more colors than most."

"How many cones do I have?"

"Most people have three. Your dad didn't even know he had the extra one until college."

"What did it let him do?"

"I guess he could see millions of more colors than the average person. You know your dad always wanted to be a painter?" Walter does not remember this. "When you were younger, I would always do craft projects with you all, except when it came to painting. Then Dad took over."

"Did he ever paint anything for you?"

"Sure, plenty of things," Elizabeth says, traveling back in time.

"How come he worked at the car place then?"

"Well, when we had your brother, we had to make some practical decisions. Money, health insurance, those became important things in our life."

"Did he still want to be a painter, even after all of us were born?"

"I think so. You know when kids are really little, like your sister's age, everyone basically wants to be one of three or four things when they grow up, but when you get to be around Mitchell's age, you realize there are more possibilities. And even if you don't end up being that thing from that age, it still probably always hangs out in the back of your mind."

"Did you always want to be a librarian?"

"I always wanted to work with books, especially children's books, so, in a way, I guess I did."

"Do you think Dad was ever angry that he couldn't be a painter?"

"No. Definitely no. He was going to be an artist, but he got to be a dad instead. I don't think he would have traded that for anything."

These are the moments when Elizabeth misses her husband the most. While it pains to speak about him, she knows the more she does, the more it keeps him around. She is aware that there is a certain detachment for Walter that comes with the subject of his dad. It is not his fault. He will naturally forget more and more every year. When a child loses a loved one, each day removed from their life increasingly obscures their memory. It starts with forgetting their voice and moves to impressions informed primarily by pictures. In Elizabeth's recent despair, Walter's disappearance brought forth the idea that even if he did return home one day, if that day was many days away, would he have begun to forget about her?

"You know, Mom, I know you don't believe about my powers, but that's okay. I don't want anyone to believe them."

"What do you mean?"

"What if that's all people want from me? What if someone bad wants to use me again?"

"Then don't tell anyone. Either way, it doesn't have to define you. Who knows about it right now?"

"Not many, I guess. Do we have to tell the police?"

"You don't want to?"

"No."

"Why not?"

"How can we be sure that they're good?"

"Officer Burton seemed like she was."

"But how can we be sure they *all* are?" Walter got the sense from both George and Jamie that Stone was the last level of a video game kind of villain, and he knows you do not get to be at the last level without picking up a few allies.

"Okay. Then we don't have to. Plus, maybe your visions will go away anyway."

"Maybe. Did Dad ever stop seeing all the colors?

"I'm not sure. We didn't talk about it much. There were other things that were more important."

"Like what?"

"Like you, your brother, your sister." Elizabeth notices Walter taking his turn in the time machine. "Sweetheart, are you sure you're ready to go back to school? I'm sure your teachers would understand if you stayed home a few more days."

"No, I want to go back."

"You do?"

"Yeah, I do. Sometimes you just got to deal with the hard stuff."

***

In the three months since Walter's second first day of fifth grade, there was a field trip with no issues and eight weeks with minimal anxiety. That streak was broken when Walter was assigned a current events article and opened *The Sacramento Bee* to read, "Park To Be Named in Honor of Slain Homeless Advocate Stone Archer."

The story detailed the coming construction of a park that would feature a boat launch and picnic grounds situated in the heart of the soon-to-be-renovated waterfront district. Aside from the shock of this news, the Crane household has settled down. Any woman with sunglasses that might seek to tie up loose ends is miles away in seclusion along the Truckee River, as content as can be. Archer's assassin was never apprehended and is rumored to be studying at a school of mystics in Kashmir.

It is November in the capital city, and Aunt Carol is prepping a record number of orders for Thanksgiving cornucopias. Officer Burton has recently returned a missing 7-month-old to her mom and dad three days before the holiday; meanwhile, Elizabeth finds herself slowly recovering when she is forced to reckon with the anniversary of her husband's death.

It is the start of Thanksgiving break when the family loads into the car for their trip to East Lawn Mortuary. Fall days in Sacramento like to start frigid and end up in the vicinity of warm. This bothers both Crane boys because the weather forces them to wear layers to school that become burdens by lunchtime. Walter has had enough this morning, as he is intentionally without a jacket.

"Walter, jacket," Elizabeth succinctly instructs.

"It will get hot. It always does," Walter counters.

"Everyone's bringing a jacket. You need one too."

"Walter, look, it's so spark-e-ly," Annie exclaims, showing off her new sequined zip-up.

"Mom, let him. It's not like he's going to get kidnapped or something," Mitchell jokes. Elizabeth is not sure she is ready for this particular brand of humor, but it does help put things in perspective.

"Fine, get in the car. I hope you don't get cold."

"Thanks. And I promise I won't get cold or kidnapped." Even Walter has joined in the fun.

When the quartet arrives at the cemetery, the mood changes. An apprehensive silence takes over as they pass through the large black gates and onto the road that rolls past tombstones and mausoleums. One year ago, the Cranes sat in a front pew in St. Francis Church. Aunt Carol bounced Annie on her thigh, Walter consoled his mom with a tight hug, and Mitchell cried uncontrollably at seeing his father carried out in a sleek copper casket. Mitchell is riding shotgun now and keeps his eyes trained on the center of the grounds, where he knows his father lies. Walter is in the back with Annie, who is generally unaware of where they are, except that she is "going to see my daddy."

Walter has not spoken in five minutes. Not only can he feel the outside chill sneak in through his window, but he finds the cemetery unsettling. For him, it represents the worst-case scenario in anyone's life. It is the one thing that is not manageable. You can come back from a fender bender or a trip to the hospital, but the cemetery operates in a one-way direction. Trips here are inevitable and, in his experience, sudden, as his dad's passing confirmed his worst fears. Walter has practiced calming strategies in the days leading up to today, but there is not a stress ball as powerful as the promise of death that now surrounds him.

After locating the burial site, the Crane children begin their tasks. Mitchell commands the spray solution and rag that clean his father's plaque. Annie is in charge of laying flowers, while Walter places a pinwheel in the ground in front. A crisp breeze begins blowing the pinwheel immediately. Standing back, Elizabeth gathers her three kids, shuts her eyes, and takes a breath. Walter is close to her, hands deep in his pockets and nestled next to her for the warmth he will not admit he needs.

Walter, we are going to kill you.

During his time with George and Jamie, Walter was always focused on the *will-I-or-won't-I* of returning home. He has only recently realized how close to death he was. The breeze picks up. Elizabeth holds her family tightly. Mitchell's eyes gather moisture while Annie plays with her shiny jacket accessories. The breeze knocks over the pinwheel, and Walter leaves the coziness of his mom's coat to fix the fallen graveside decor. As Walter kneels, his leg is made wet by the remnants of the morning dew. He picks up the pinwheel with his right hand and steadies himself on his dad's plaque with his left. The inscription is so close, his dad so close. He hears his brother sobbing in the background. The wind graduates beyond a breeze. Then one of those things happens—it just happens. No one notices but Walter.

A wince. Walter's weight falls on his left hand as his eyelids lock down. A burst of light enters his field of vision, and then the flickering starts to piece together. At first, there is no world around him, but Walter soon sees it. He does not believe it, but it is there. Or, rather, it is what is *not* there that is important. *Gone*. When the flickering stabilizes, he can see everything: the casket beneath him, lined in velvet, empty, as it has been for the past year. Walter's eyes open.

THE END